PERFECT KISS

~A NIGHT TO REMEMBER . . .
A PROM TO FORGET~

Robin Mellom

ISBN-13: 9781508563204

A PROLOGUE, I SUPPOSE

Food, a cell phone, and my dignity . . . all things I do not have

I DON'T KNOW how I ended up on the side of Hollister Road, lying in this ditch.

This moment, last night, the details—all fuzzy. A reluctant glance down and I see I'm covered in scratches and bruises. The bruise on my shin appears to be in the shape of a french fry. French fries cause bruises? And I have at least seven stains on my royal blue iridescent dress—two black, one greenish-bluish, and the remaining are various shades of yellow. *What are these? Mustard? Curry?*

Wait. I don't even want to know.

What I *do* want to know is why I just fell out of a moving Toyota Prius and was left here in this ditch with a french fry shin bruise and unrecognizable stains. Especially the yellow ones.

Please, please be curry.

Looking down the road, I see two things: the sun coming up behind Hollister Peak, and the car lights on Brian Sontag's Prius getting smaller and smaller in the distance.

The jerk.

I start to think about last night, but the past twelve hours are a total blur. Like, for instance, how and *why* I got into Brian Sontag's Toyota Prius.

I touch my forehead, which is already swelling from the fall, and I realize this must be why I can't remember a thing from last night. I look down at myself again and wish I hadn't. Gross. If Ian could see me now, he would ditch me for sure.

Except that he already has.

I even wore blue for him. Not all black, as usual. It was an actual *color*. Not that I wanted to wear it—but I guess even wearing something that went against my better fashion sense couldn't change his mind.

You are now officially on my list, Ian Clark. And not the good one.

The conversation. I suddenly remember the conversation we had two weeks ago.

"It will be amazing," he said. "I can't wait to walk into that room with you," he said. "It will be the best night of our lives," he said, as if he were reading straight from a Hallmark card.

So I told him I would go. I even told him if a Journey song came on, I would dance with him, and I imagined my arms draped around his neck, and his breath on my cheek, and my hip brushing up against his. I didn't explain I had been imagining a lot of things about him lately.

He made fun of me for organizing all the special moments in my life like I was a professional wedding planner. "The toast will happen here . . . the dance will happen here . . . and voilà! Happiness!"

That's when I punched him on the arm.

But he was right, actually—I did have that special moment all planned out . . . the kiss, of course . . . that kiss. Every detail of our first kiss that I hoped—hoped beyond measure—would finally happen between us. And change everything.

I even hoped that when we kissed, we'd be standing next to beautiful lush foliage. And a water feature. It's possible I've watched one too many romance movies.

But so much for acts of extreme hoping. Look at me now. There is nothing special about this moment. No foliage, nothing lush—just dried weeds and gravel burrowing into my legs. And butt, honestly.

The glamour of this moment is stunning. Thank God my lovely sense of sarcasm is still intact. It feels like the only thing that is.

There's an aching pain on my right upper arm. It's because of the tattoo. Wait, I have a tattoo? Who let me get a tattoo?! It's a Tinker Bell. Which could be cute if it weren't for the fact that she's a *punk* Tinker Bell. She's wearing combat boots, her wings are ripped, and her eyes are bloodshot. Great . . . Tinker Bell on a meth binge.

I stare up to the heavens.

Please, please be temporary.

I wipe the dirt from my face and shake my head. I can remember every detail of that conversation two weeks ago, but I can't remember a thing about the past twelve hours. Seriously?

A couple of deep breaths and I accept that I am now keenly aware of only three things:

1. It is 6:15 in the morning and I am a heap of a mess sitting in a ditch on the side of Hollister Road. I know this because my watch—the one that matches my dress and purse and shoes (thank you, Mom)—is still ticking despite the impact. *Ouch . . . my head hurts.* And I know it's Hollister Road because this is the back road that Ian always uses on the way to school when there's construction. I'd recognize that billboard anywhere. The one that says "Peg Griffith— Philanthropist of the Year!" and Peg is holding a metal statue in the shape of a heart. And Ian always asks, "Doesn't your mom get queasy around all that blood?" And I always answer, "She's a philanthropist, not a phlebotomist." And he lets out that sweet, goofy laugh that gives me butterflies. I hate this stupid road.

2. I still don't remember anything that happened last night.

3. I am starving.

My forehead is pounding, and I grab it, but it's not the pain I'm trying to stop; it's the memories that suddenly come rushing in.

Oh, no. No, no, no. The dinner. The dance. Allyson Moore. Jimmy Choo heels. That broken safety pin. In-N-Out Burger. Tinker Bell. The Hampton Inn. The three-legged Chihuahua. Brian Sontag. Toyota Prius. Ian Clark.

Ian, who brought me a blue corsage, dyed to match my dress (and shoes and purse and watch).

Ian, who bought me a Mrs. Fields peanut butter cookie and stashed it in his glove compartment because he knew I would need a snack at some point in the night, given my low blood sugar problem. And my love of peanut butter cookies.

Ian, who promised we would dance to our song. Who promised prom night would be the best night of my life—his Hallmark promises.

And I believed him.

I glance around, looking for cars. But it's a Sunday. No traffic. No one to take pity on me and drive me home. Or at least lend me their cell phone so I can call my mom.

Mom!

She's going to kill me. I was supposed to be home by two a.m.! She must be panicked. But then again, she's probably asleep. It's going to be okay. Mom is a deep sleeper. People who do good deeds sleep very well.

And, oh man, she trusted him. "I wouldn't feel good about Justina going to prom with anyone but you," Mom had said. She even dusted off his tuxedo sleeve when she said it. And he gave that laugh.

I hate stupid tuxedo sleeves.

I have to get out of here. Find a phone. Something, *someone* to help me. I push myself up off the ground, but the sudden movement causes my head to swirl and I feel light- headed. Low blood sugar—it always makes me dizzy. And grumpy. And yes, even irrational. But right now, I'm entitled.

I take a slow breath, and the balance comes back. I put one foot in front of the other and manage to hobble down the road. But my feet are heavy, clunky, like submarines in a sea of taffy.

I need help. Where is Anderson Cooper when I need him?

Of course I know Ian would laugh at that if he could hear me. And yeah, maybe I should be obsessed with a hot musician or a movie star. But crushing on a CNN news reporter just makes more sense.

I'm into reliability, Ian.

Plus, Anderson Cooper's totally cute. I don't mind the ears.

But even *he's* not here. No one is. The road is deserted. I'm going to have to figure out a way to get out of this myself.

I'm going to pray for a miracle.

Please, please be erased. Make Worst Night Ever slip away from my brain.

But luckily, before I get too far in my pleading and have to start kneeling and ruining this dress any further . . . I see them. In the distance are familiar glistening fluorescent lights. I smile because I know those lights mean I have found the answer to all my problems.

A pay phone and a candy bar at the 7-Eleven.

Chapter One

FINALLY, A SNICKERS

I SUPPOSE IF I have to get ditched somewhere, I'm glad it's at *this* 7-Eleven, not the sucky 7-Eleven near downtown. This is the awesome one—the one on 4th and Hill with the nacho cheese bar and the endless row of magazines. Ian and I would stop by here on Fridays to celebrate. "No homework. No track practice. Time for jalapeño nachos!" he would always say. And I'd say, "Just a Snickers."

It's not that I don't love nachos . . . what's not to love? But I never got them on our Friday 7-Eleven stops because that was the day my weekly thimble-sized allowance was hovering in the cents column, and a candy bar was all I could afford. Ian would've bought nachos for me—he's a carefree buyer with an unlimited allowance, along with most of the student body at Huntington High School, but I didn't want him to worry that it symbolized more. The last thing I wanted was to weird out our friendship because of a plate of convenience-store nachos.

As I cross through the familiar gas station parking lot, my chest discovers gravity, and my organs and bones weigh me down with sadness, my feet barely moving forward.

Of all the 7-Elevens, *this* one.

Where are you, Ian Clark?

Then music. It's blaring through outdoor speakers, which seems odd this early in the morning. There's no one to listen to it because there are no customers. Except for me.

The bell rings as the sliding glass door opens and a gush of stale air-conditioned air rushes over me. Country music blasts through the indoor speakers, too.

"Need something?"

The cashier stares at my shoes. My two-and-three- quarter-inch heels are covered in dirt and mud—the same ones I had proudly dyed iridescent royal blue just two days ago. But that was before I found out *nobody* dyes their shoes to match their dress anymore. And before I realized listening to the advice of a relative—not my best friend and not an enlightened editor of a prom magazine—was an unwise idea.

Thank you, Mom.

It makes sense that the cashier would stare. I'm guessing not too many girls waltz into the 7-Eleven at 6:15 on a Sunday morning wearing heels that match their shimmering iridescent blue dress, looking like they'd just lost a match with a vindictive sewer rat.

"Got any Snickers?" My voice is weak.

Her eyes drift up to mine. She softens. She must notice my extreme lack of lip gloss. "You hungry?" She looks over my shoulder, probably to see if I am alone.

"Very."

She is wearing high-waisted jeans, a belt with a large silver buckle, and a long-sleeve white shirt tucked tightly into her jeans. Her ultra-long hair is pulled back in a perfect French braid—totally symmetrical—with hints of gray peeking through. She looks like she belongs in a music video for the country song playing over the speakers. Like she'd play the part of the consoling wise aunt who doles out good obvious advice: *Stop drinkin' and smokin' and bringing home stray dogs, honey!*

I can already tell I like her.

She reaches into a box in front of the counter and lays a jumbo-size Snickers on the counter. I was right—there really is kindness in the world. I glance at her nametag.

"Thanks, Gilda."

I give her a big smile and reach for the candy bar. "That's $1.09," she says. "I...I..." I can't believe Gilda isn't going to take some pity on me. Do I look like a monster?

I keep my mouth shut about her lack of human decency, and pat my dress down as if my purse will suddenly appear. But it's gone and I have no idea where I left it. Of course all my money is in there. And my lip gloss. And those directions to Lurch's party. The one Ian and I were supposed to go to the next night. He said he wanted us to go do something fun, just to make sure there wasn't any weirdness after prom. He even said *weirdness* with air quotes, like I didn't know what it meant. I had hoped "weirdness" referred to all the kissing we were going to do—so I guess I didn't know what it meant.

I had no idea "weirdness" to him meant actual weirdness. Dang it.

But in thinking over what happened last night, I have to say, "weirdness" was an understatement of epic proportion. Unreasonably huge . . . an understatement that is Hummer huge. Because Lurch's party—and especially the excessive kissing part—is *never* going to happen.

Which is a pity. Lurch always has the best parties.

"I don't have any money." My voice cracks. It sounds pitiful. Like someone you might even want to take mercy on. But it doesn't sway Gilda.

Gilda places the Snickers back in its box. Then she looks me up and down and tilts her head. "You need a phone or something?"

"Yes! Where?" I feel like a Jack Russell terrier—yippy, anxious.

"Out back. By the hoses. Fifty cents a call."

I'm not exactly sure why she thinks I can suddenly come up with fifty cents if I couldn't afford the Snickers. "Thanks." I wince at her. All I really want is to get home, so I retreat and hobble back through the sliding glass doors, across the parking lot.

The pay phone is *right* next to the hoses, just like Sorta Rude Gilda said, and I have to hike up my disgusting dress to get around them. I'm not sure why I care about saving my dress from any further grossness. This is absurd.

As I step up to the phone, I hear a car—the rattling, knocking sound of a diesel engine. I whip around, hoping it's Ian, but deep down knowing that he's never coming to get me. A man pulls up in a Mercedes to pump gas. His car is old, just like Ian's, but it's a coupe, not a sedan. He doesn't even notice me. Good.

I start to read the directions on the pay phone, but the words turn blurry. I can feel the tears gaining momentum—I press my temples with my palms, trying my best to contain them.

Get it together. You've gotten this far without falling apart.

My pep talk starts to work—the tears dry up and I glance back at the building to see Gilda planted at the window, glaring at me with her arms folded, standing firm like a redwood tree. She must think I'm going to steal these hoses. Gilda might be the type who takes her job too seriously.

I quickly turn back and finish reading the directions on how to make a collect call. I've never made one and it looks complicated.

I dial wrong three times, but then finally push all the right buttons in the right order and the phone rings.

Come on, Mom. Pick up.

"You've reached the Griffith residence. Please leave a message. . . ."

I can't believe this. She's still asleep. Doesn't she know I'm not there? No, this can't be right. Maybe she's out on a hunt with the police. They're probably using drug-sniffing dogs and everything. Given the people I've been hanging out with the past few hours, those drug dogs will sniff me out for sure. Should be rescued any moment now. . .

But I try the collect call one more time. "You've reached the Griffith residence . . ."

This can't be happening. She's asleep. She doesn't even know Ian just ruined my life. I never wanted to go to this stupid prom at that stupid hotel. I told him that: I like running, not dancing. I like veggie burritos, not rubbery hotel chicken. And definitely not rubbery hotel salad. But he convinced me that prom would be different. It would be a night I would never forget, and he promised I'd love the food. Well, he was right about one thing: I will *never* forget this. But the food? I'm freaking starving. All of a sudden, I can't hold the tears back anymore, my eyes feeling like the Colorado River after a spring melt—the flow just keeps coming. No pep talk can fix this. I fall to the ground, sobbing.

Why me, Ian? Why couldn't you have—

"Eat this."

There's a tap on my shoulder. Gilda drops a Snickers on my lap.

She reaches out and gives me a hand, helping me to my feet. "Here." It's a scratchy paper towel from the bathroom— she motions to the tears flowing freely down my face, and I wish she had brought more scratchy towels.

I try to explain, not really sure what to say, and the words come out as a blubbering mess. "Why did you . . . Are you—"

"You look like you could use a snack. That's all." She leads me back to the store. "Come inside. We'll figure out what to do with you."

I knew there was kindness in the world. Sometimes I guess you have to turn into the Colorado Snot River before someone shows it, but I'm just relieved to know it's there.

Gilda pulls a stool up to the end of the counter and lets me sit while I scarf down my candy bar. She takes a plastic to-go bag and fills it with ice from the soda machine, then spins the bag to close it and hands it to me. "What happened to you, anyway?"

I hold the ice to the knot on my head. *Ouch!*

She waits a moment. "So?"

I look down at my dress. "You mean the stains?"

She nods. "And the scratches and the bruises and the bump on the head and the new tattoo."

I shake my head. "I know. So cliché to go to prom and end up with a tattoo, right?"

"That's your *prom* dress?"

"It looked better without the filth."

Her face is blank. "It's just all so . . . *matching*. I thought maybe you'd been in a play. Or a pride parade." I almost laugh—like she even knows what a pride parade is, but I don't feel a need to educate her on this matter. "Nope. Mom's idea."

"You didn't get a friend's opinion?"

I shake my head. "Didn't even read a magazine. I just wanted to impress him—"

"With your matching skills?"

"Color. But Mom dressed me exactly the way she did at her own prom . . . secondhand dress, dyed shoes, matching purse." I lower my head. "It's not like I'm proud of this."

Of course I would much rather be wearing my regular clothes: all-black everything, as Ian calls them. True, I only wear black: black shirt, black jeans, black boots, every day, without fail. Because no one asks questions. They just assume I've gone to the dark side— and lately that would not be too far from the truth.

But I get wild sometimes—with my nail polish. Black Cherry.

Gilda gives me a look like she's in pain—physical pain. "You mean you let your *mother* dress you the same way she dressed for prom?"

She must not have a daughter. Otherwise she'd understand how hard it is for a mother to let her daughter just "be." At least for *my* mother. I consider explaining this to her, but I figure I should zip it and be thankful for the Snickers. Plus, the rush of chocolate is calming me down, and the balance of blood sugar suddenly makes me a much more reasonable person. Unlike most of last night.

I shrug. "Mom's eager face—there's no escaping it."

Gilda scratches her hair, digging in delicately with her long red fingernails, being careful not to mess up a braid. I can tell she wants to let loose with some sort of hand-flailing lecture on being myself and not letting my mother's eager face control my life, but all she says is, "Huh."

I take another bite of my Snickers and swallow hard. Here comes the energy. "Look, if I had known my dress was going to cause this much pain, I would've worn a sleeping bag. No . . . I wouldn't have gone at all."

She narrows her eyes. "Spill it then. Why'd you go?"

Of course that's when his face pops into my mind. And all the amazing things he said to convince me to go to prom.

"Ian Clark," I say, as if that explains everything. But she doesn't know him. How could she understand his powers of persuasion?

Gilda looks around the store. "Ian Clark isn't here now. Did he do something bad?"

"Yeah. Very bad."

"Did he—"

"Hurt me?" I ask, because, looking at me, I'd wonder too.

She wrinkles her nose. I can tell she doesn't want to ask, but she knows she should. "Did he?"

"No, no. He ditched me." I adjust the ice pack on my forehead. The pain is lessening. I'm starting to think more clearly. "I was ditched. Figuratively and literally."

"He sounds like a real jerk."

I twitch. That word: *jerk*. It confuses my nervous system because my body wants to react with my first instinct . . . defend him.

Because even though *jerk* is the only word I can imagine to describe him now, it's not a word that ever entered my mind as being synonymous with Ian Clark. Ever.

I have always known *of* him—Huntington High isn't huge and it's the type of place where everyone's business is just known. It's almost as if we're all distant relatives— people you've heard of and you know their basic story—or the Lifetime movie version of their story—but you don't *really* know them.

Ian became more than a person I knew basic facts about back in sophomore year, spring quarter, P.E.: softball. I remember my first words to him. "Have you seen that silver bat around?"

He turned and walked off on me. Sorta rude. But then he popped back into my vision a moment later, the bat in hand. "Silver bat's my favorite too." He gave it to me, but not in just some ordinary handing-over-of-a-bat type of way. He flipped it around in a highly coordinated maneuver and presented it to me, handle first. Just to make it that much easier for me. "Whack it good," he said with a little smile.

I struck out.

But I stuffed that little moment away in my mind— the importance of it seeming like something that needed to be noted, filed, remembered. I now knew Ian Clark was a handle-first kind of guy. Why did this matter to me?

But time passed and the silver bat always seemed to be around and I couldn't think of any other questions to ask him. So I didn't. And that memory started to fade. Ian remained merely an unexamined file in my brain.

Until last summer. The pool party.

Gilda opens up a bag of gummy bears and chews the head off of one, then hands a piece to me, an indication she's ready for the story. "Why'd you go with this guy?"

I twirl the gummy bear in my fingers. "Operation Lips Locked."

"What type of operation is that?"

Breathe in. Breathe out. Here we go.

"It's the type where you get ridiculed at Jimmy DeFranco's pool party for hooking up with two different guys even though it was accidental because one of them was a dare and one of them was due to drinking too many Jägermeister shots—him, not me—and get publicly humiliated when those two guys claim it was much more than kissing—which is all you remember happening—but the glares from people you hardly know pierce your skin and jab your heart, so you declare to your best friend you are never *ever* going to kiss another boy again until you know deep in your bones, in your marrow, in your cell structure—one hundred percent—that he is boyfriend material."

"Okay," Gilda says. "I mean . . . *what?*"

I shrug. "No kissing allowed until the guy proved he had the material. Until then, lips locked." I press my lips together, reminding myself what they feel like. "It's been eight months and twelve days since I kissed a boy. I was going to finally unlock my lips for Ian. At prom."

The bell at the sliding door rings. The man who was pumping gas in the old Mercedes strolls around the store.

Gilda holds her hand up to me and whispers, "Hold on a sec."

She helps him find some individual packets of Tylenol, then rings him up. He's older with a pudgy middle and a rumpled shirt.

While he fishes through his leather wallet for money, he glances my way. And as he hands Gilda a twenty, he's still looking my way.

I shift on my stool. What's this guy's problem? "You need a lift?" he asks.

I laugh. A nervous laugh. Not really a laugh. "Me? No." "Her ride's coming," Gilda lies.

He puts his wallet away and gives me a smirk. "Looks like you worked a rough shift last night. Hope you made enough to buy yourself a new dress."

Oh my god, the guy thinks I'm a—oh, I can't even . . .

He scoops up his bag of Tylenol—hangover medicine, I'm sure—and saunters out before I can tell him he's so rude for assuming something I'm NOT. I'm only sixteen and this is my prom dress and my boyfriend who is not my boyfriend ditched me, and no, I do *not* have a ride home!

But I've gotten good at not confronting people. I let out a deep sigh instead.

When he's gone, Gilda turns to me with big eyes. "He doesn't know you haven't even kissed a boy in eight months. He's a jerk."

I shake my head, thinking about school and the reputation I managed to create for myself. "He's probably not totally off base. I've kissed a lot of guys in my past."

She waves me off. "Oh, who hasn't."

"A lot." I clear my throat and hope she doesn't ask—

"How many?"

Of course she asks. I clench my fists and look away. "A little more than a dozen." Silence, no response. "Or so," I add quietly.

"Or *so*?!" Her eyes are satellite disks.

"It's not like it's triple digits or anything. And it's not something I'm super proud of, except at first . . . I kind of . . . was."

Which is true. When I first started my excessive lip landings, I was a freshman and I was so excited about my success rate I wanted to put it on my résumé—in bold, italics, everything. I was *proud.*

"But nothing ever materialized. No boyfriend," I explain to her. "I just really, really like kissing. But now it's like I have a kissing disorder—I've overdosed on it and now I can't even get one simple smooch from my prom date. I mean, it's *prom. Everyone* gets kissed on prom night! What is wrong with me?" I look down at my muddy feet.

I feel like a non-human at this point. Realizing that it's come to this. Me without any dignity—completely alone and thinking only about the feel of his lips—and he's probably off with Allyson Moore doing whatever he's doing. I take a breath and look up at Gilda. "I'm always The Girl At That Party, never The Girl."

"Sounds like you've kissed one too many toads."

"And toads never turn into boyfriends. Not in my case."

"But Ian proved he was boyfriend material?"

"Yeah. Except it took a long time for me to realize it. We were . . . friends. For a long time. Like, almost nine months. I mean, that's how long it takes to incubate a baby, or whatever." I take a bite of the gummy bear, feeling more settled. "Ian drove me to school every day. And he'd remind me which color uniform I needed for a track meet. I trusted him." I stare at the half-eaten gummy bear, getting lost in the memories of him. "It's strange how you can be friends with someone for so long and then one day he brings you licorice and Motrin because you're whacked out from heinous painful cramps straight from the devil, but you notice he's wearing a new shirt that's a certain shade of green and . . . whammo! Your insides turn to pudding and all you can do is think about kissing him. He's the same guy, doesn't change a bit from one day to the next"—I start to think about his eyes, his mouth—"but because a color brings out his eyes, you suddenly realize . . ."

Gilda finishes my sentence. "Boyfriend material."

I sigh. "Totally."

That green shirt. None of this would have happened if it weren't for that stupid color. It's like some nightmare *Sesame Street* episode: *This month's gut-wrenching, painful heartache brought to you by the color green!*

But I quickly snap back to reality and remind myself that I am telling this story to the cashier at the 7-Eleven due to the fact that Ian Clark left me on prom night and I ended up in a ditch on Hollister Road.

Screw the color green.

I sit up and clear my throat. "He totally *was* boyfriend material. At least I never kissed the guy."

"That's good. I guess."

Maybe Gilda is right. It is good we never kissed. That way we don't have to worry about any "weirdness." Except that our friendship has come to a complete halt, and I'll have to find a new ride to school. Which is a total pain. So I should've just kissed him and gotten something out of this ridiculous mess. Plus, I still can't help but wonder what it would've been like.

Curse you, wonder.

"Or maybe I should've kissed him. Just once? Like maybe I should've done it a long time ago, not sat around waiting for the perfect moment. I could've gotten it out of the way."

"Like a chore?"

I laugh at that. I've never thought of kissing as a chore. More of a sport. "I just don't want to have to wonder anymore."

"Wonder what?"

"If he's the perfect kisser. Some guys are—they know exactly how much tongue to give, when to be gentle, and when to put on the deep pressure."

She quickly pops another gummy bear in her mouth and fake coughs.

"Sorry. Too much?" I wince.

She gazes off in the distance toward the hot-dog cooker. "No. Actually, I know exactly what you mean."

I snag another handful of bears from the bag and start gnawing. It really seems to calm the nerves. "Okay then, so you know that there are also guys who are awful kissers. Too wet. Too toothy. Too much tongue. Too much breathing. Too much coloring outside the lines, you know what I mean? I want to know which category he falls in."

"You still want to know?"

Immediately I picture him talking to Allyson Moore next to that pool and then overhearing that phone conversation in the In-N-Out Burger bathroom. "No. Not anymore. All Ian Clark got me was a ruined dress. And the worst night of my life." I straighten out my stained dress.

Allyson Moore.

Just *thinking* about her almost makes me throw up in my mouth. I mean, what was it exactly that he couldn't resist? Her strappy, silver Jimmy Choo pumps? Or her pale pink lip gloss with a hint of glitter? Surely it wasn't her remarkable intelligence—the girl thinks monogamy is a type of dark wood. Maybe he found her lack of common vocabulary terms adorable?

None of this makes sense. Ian is not the kind of guy who would leave me alone in a ditch. And somewhere deep in me, maybe in some file buried in my brain, I know this is true.

At least, I *hope* it's true.

This picture is so fuzzy . . . no crisp black and whites . . . just grays . . . and unanswered questions.

Gilda leans toward me to get a better look at my stained outfit. "What *are* all these?"

Looking them over, I realize each one tells a little piece of the story of what happened to me last night. Like a quilt—a stain quilt. A disastrous, heartbreaking, nasty stain quilt. "You really want to know?"

Gilda looks around at the empty store, another sad country song blaring in the background. She shrugs. "It's real busy, but I guess I could spare some time." She winks then tosses another gummy bear at me. "I gotta hear about this Ian Clark guy."

I point to the very first stain of the night—the one near the hem of my dress. It's the greenish-yellow one.

The one I got from him.

Chapter Two

YELLOW CURRY, EXTRA CORIANDER

IT WAS YESTERDAY. 5:30 p.m. I had just gotten back from a jog over to the CVS to pick up the perfect color of nail polish: Barbados Blue. The same color as my dress, true, but at least it wasn't Black Cherry. Tonight, I would be daring.

I had carefully instructed my mother not to answer the door with a spoon full of lentil stew or barley goop or whatever vegetable concoction she had created and force it into Ian's mouth. He might not like it. Or he might not be hungry. Or he might be nervous and not want to make small talk with my mother about how tasty the lentils were. I happened to like lentils, but—let's face it—most people think they taste like clods of dirt.

Of course Mom didn't pay attention to my request. She was making a big pot of curry. And I could sense it was going to end up in Ian's mouth.

"Why are you making me dinner?" I was still in my running clothes, crunching on a Honeycrisp apple, talking with my mouth full. "We're eating dinner at the hotel."

Mom could make a mean lentil stew, and her curry was even more amazing. She never forced me into being a vegetarian, but when I was nine I watched a science show on how things are made. Once I found out how they *really* make hot dogs, I joined her and never looked back. Meat and I formally divorced. But even though she was a fantastic vegetarian cook, it didn't mean she should force it on Ian.

She blew on the stew to cool it down, and took a bite. "It's not for you. Fundraiser tonight. Remember?"

Uh, no. I didn't remember because Mom's schedule is full of fundraisers. And committee meetings. And action planning groups. And committee meetings about the planning groups for the fundraisers, or something. It's exhausting. For me, anyway.

"Wanna taste?" Mom wasn't asking me. She was asking Sol, our chocolate Labrador retriever. She always treated him like he was royalty—like he was just as important as the President's dog, or Oprah's dog.

Sol licked the spoon, as well as all the drops on the floor. "Don't tell Daddy," she said as she patted him on the head.

I crossed my arms. "You know Dad would throw you into the backyard if he saw you feeding Sol people food."

"But he doesn't understand how much Sol loves my curry." She leaned over and whispered, "It's the extra coriander."

Since Dad was out of town, Mom was using Sol as a taste tester for her fundraiser curry instead of me, which was fortunate because it didn't do any favors for people who wanted kissable breath. It was also fortunate Dad was out of town because he wouldn't be able to greet Ian at the door and use his psychology on him.

Calm, assertive voice.

Confident stance.

No means no.

And by psychology I mean *pet psychology*. Dad calls himself "Dog Trainer to the Stars!" He once happened to meet Meryl Streep at one of Mom's fundraisers and had an impromptu dog training session with her Irish setter in the parking lot of the Hyatt. He immediately updated his résumé. Only he rarely trained celebrities' dogs; it was the hairstylist or massage therapist or dermatologist of a star who called. But because of that little line on his résumé, he now got called off to Los Angeles and Palm Springs whenever a person who knew a movie star needed dog training.

The weekend of my prom he was training Halle Berry's mani-curist's pug how to heel.

While my dad's job may sound glamorous—or not— it's not like we're rich. But we aren't poor, and we don't go without food or anything, and I always get stuff like fuzzy slippers and watches every Christmas, so there really is nothing to complain about.

But the one time I did consider complaining was a week ago when Mom took me shopping for my prom dress at a consignment shop, not the mall.

"This way, part of it will go to the person who donated the dress. Someone who *really* needs the money. It's a win- win," Mom had said.

Not that I wanted an expensive dress from the mall— it seemed like an excessive waste of money for something I was only going to wear once. But the secondhand shop didn't feel quite right either. It was fine for normal everyday clothes, but *formal* wear? Weird things happened to people dressed in formal wear, especially when worn to a party that more than likely got out of control. I couldn't be sure what that particular dress had witnessed.

I kept my mouth shut, though. Mom had a cute look on her face, and she was so excited that I'd agreed to wear a dress and not a pantsuit, which I had threatened to do.

Plus, truth be told, Ian once told me when we were sitting in the front seat of his car before school, listening to AC/DC—me decked out in black, of course, wool even, if I remember correctly—that he couldn't wait to see me in a bright, happy color someday, to match my insides. And I said it'd have to be red since my insides were sorta bloody. Then he gave that butterfly-inducing laugh.

Ian didn't know the real reason I wore black all the time.

But I liked that he wanted to see me bright and happy. So when Mom was standing in the half-off orange-dot aisle, holding a bright iridescent blue dress, wiggling with excitement and saying, "Go for the pop of color!" I gave in to her eager face.

I doubted my decision. Ever since Jimmy DeFranco's party, I doubted everything. But at least the dress didn't have a high slit that might further the reputation I couldn't seem to shake.

Maybe this dress—classic, traditional, colorful, and yeah, un-sexy—would be just the thing to remind everyone I was no longer a kissing addict. Ian might not find me super hot and sexy, and the dress was rather a failure in the good-taste department, but he'd notice the color.

He'd know I did it for him.

"Go get ready!" Mom pushed me out of the kitchen and went back to stirring her pot of fundraiser curry.

I bolted upstairs, finishing my apple just before I jumped into the shower. It was a two-minute blur. I quickly combed and dried my hair, long and straight—an expensive sleek salon updo seemed silly given all the dancing we were going to do. Plus I wanted to leave my hair wild and open for business in case Ian wanted to run his fingers through it when I laid that kiss on him. I mean, what guy would get excited about his date pulling her hair back tight and shellacking it with hair spray? It'd be like kissing a dodgeball.

I quickly slathered the Barbados Blue on my nails. I was fast, but I was accurate. The nail drying—*that's* what took time. I paced around my room and blew on my nails. *Dry, come on, dry.*

My bedroom looks like a museum dedicated to daisies. I have daisy wallpaper, daisy pillows, even the trim on my lamp shade has a daisy print. I happen to love flowers, any flower, but I *adore* ones that symbolize something. Like how lilies represent friendship. And a tulip means forgiveness. Or how a rose is supposed to mean love. Except that I hate roses. Maybe because love is too complicated to express with just a flower.

Or maybe because I don't like red or pink.

Or maybe because Ian's ex-girlfriend, Eva, was wearing a rose in her hair the night she cheated on him—yeah, at that pool party at Jimmy DeFranco's. It was an epic night, that's for sure. Ian caught

Eva making out with Jimmy in his parents' bedroom. She ran after him wearing a pink bikini, the rose in her hair flopping around, about to jump ship. "It was only a kiss!" she screamed. But he dumped her. Wouldn't even give her a chance to explain.

That was the first night we talked about more than silver bats. My darkest moment. And his too. I was outside on the curb, crying because guys were saying they heard I was making the rounds. The jerks. Jason Harper was my only intentional kissing act that night, but Aaron Becker, drunk on Jägermeister shots, dragged me by my elbow to show me a dent he'd gotten in his dad's BMW but instead stopped me in the hallway and gave me an unsolicited hard sloppy kiss. I actually had to stomp on his toe to get him away from me. Thank God his toes were vulnerable in those flip-flops. And then all I could do was run.

So next thing I knew, Ian had plopped down next to me on the curb, right after Eva had taken off sobbing. "Epic night, huh?" he said with sarcasm, but it was the sad kind, not the rude kind, and I instantly felt at ease.

I looked him over and remembered who he was: the handle-first guy. I wiped my face. "I'm never kissing another boy again."

"O-kay. I'm Ian."

"I know. I remember you," I said. "I hate boys. You included. You should probably know that up front."

He nodded. "And I hate girls."

We shook hands, and that was it. We were perfect together.

As friends.

Months went by. We were friends and then even better friends. We carpooled. We shared history notes. We drove around and screamed AC/DC songs. Then we talked about the important things.

"Seriously, Lay's are the best," I'd say.

"Ruffles, you goof."

"Texture?"

"Yeah," he'd say. "There's something *there*. Something to hold on to."

"So you don't like *flat* things?" I'd wiggle my chest, strangely unafraid around him to be proud of my less-than-impressive chest.

"Are we comparing chips to the female form?"

"I don't know." I'd squint my eyes. "Are we?"

"Yes, Justina. That makes perfect sense. I only eat Ruffles because they make me think of a girl's chest, and I'm the type of guy to base my food preferences on girly parts. I prefer grapefruit to apples, you know."

"And the truth comes out."

We always teetered on the edge of flirtation—delicately dipping our toes in, but never fully plunging. That was the best part of our friendship, the unsaid part—the playful looks, the teetering, the toe-dips.

But there was one part of his friendship I couldn't live without.

When we took our conversation to the point of "almost too far," he'd pause, his face would flush, and he'd pull up the right side of his mouth into a smirk. No words, just a smirk. And it was then—when his mouth was pulled up to the right—that the most heavenly, lovely, tiny crease would appear.

That crease.

It made me drunk.

And what he didn't know—or maybe he did—was that I spent most of my time figuring out how to get another one.

That crease became air—I needed it.

But I think he loved the feel of that elusive crease on his own face just as much as I loved looking at it.

Even with all that delicate toe-dipping, I kept to my promise and didn't come close to locking lips with him for a long, long time. Having Ian for a friend was just what I needed.

But everything changed in an instant when he brought me licorice and Motrin, wearing that green shirt. But I never told him. I just kept treating him like a friend and silently imagining us being so much more.

After his breakup with Eva, it took him eight months before he got up enough nerve to ask another girl out.

Me.

And even though we were only friends, I couldn't help but hope he'd asked because he wanted to be more. But then again, maybe I was just a distraction from a rose-loving girl like Eva.

All I knew was, to me, roses couldn't handle the weight of their symbolism. But a daisy never took on more than it could handle. It was a simple flower. It wasn't complicated. And it symbolized more than just "Peace, man." It meant innocence . . . gentleness.

Ian Clark was all daisy.

Nails finally dry, I leaned in to my mirror and took an extra moment to pile on the lip gloss. Attached to my mirror was the invitation Ian had left for me in my locker. Of course it had a daisy taped to it. He was persuasive in *many* ways.

The Senior Class of Huntington High School
request the honor of your presence at the Junior/Senior Prom
on Saturday, April Fifteenth at Eight O'clock in the evening
The Grand Riverside Hotel

"The Grand Riverside Hotel," I said out loud with an accent dripping with royalness as I looked at myself in the bathroom mirror. I couldn't wait to walk into that ballroom with Ian. And I was wearing a sparkly, iridescent blue dress that matched the bright happiness of my insides (my emotional inside part, not my bloody inside part).

He'd better notice, because everything about tonight was going to be different.

I hadn't had the guts to tell him that my feelings had changed since green shirt day. But hopefully a kiss would do the talking for me. For some reason, I just couldn't say the words. Maybe that's what had happened to him the day he'd asked me.

"It'll be amazing," he had said. "No, um, pressure. We'll just . . ."

"Just what?" I'd leaned in and caught his eyes to get him to finish his sentence.

"We'll go . . . as friends."

"Friends."

"Right?"

He'd winced when he said it. He wanted *me* to decide?

"Right." The word came out without thought, and I'd regretted it the second it fell out of my mouth. This had been my opening to tell him how I felt, all laid out before me like a red carpet. But the words hadn't come for either of us—just a lot of wincing and throat clearing and shirt readjusting.

That's when I decided it was *action* that was going to take this to the next level. Not words.

I knew that the kiss I was going to give him was like putting all my cards on the table. I didn't know if he felt the same way—maybe he really did want to just be friends, which meant this could all end badly.

But oh, lordy, that green shirt.

He was worth the risk.

I'd imagined—in great detail—that we would kiss for the first time at night under and umbrella...the droplets of rain twinkling in the city lights, looking like stars falling all around us.

But we lived in California and the odds of us locking lips for the first time in the rain was less than eight percent, according to Steve The Man, Channel 7 meteorologist.

So prom would have to do. It was the perfect Plan B.

"Are you ready, Justina?" Mom called out. "Let me see your dress!" She was getting anxious.

So was I.

I slipped my shoes on, the ones Mom had convinced me to dye blue, and I spent a moment staring at my outfit, now all finally pulled together.

Wow. I suddenly felt overwhelmingly . . . blue.

I decided I would show Mom the dress before Ian got there—let her get all her overbearing giddiness out of the way. But it didn't turn out that way, because he was standing in the kitchen when I walked in, and there was my mother, cupping her hand under his chin, trying to stuff him with fundraiser curry.

"The secret is extra coriander," she was explaining.

I quietly stepped into the room and cleared my throat. I had hoped for some smiles, maybe some hugs and a gorgeous flower corsage—a daisy, of course. But the overwhelming color of my dress and matching shoes must have taken them both by surprise, because Ian threw his hands in the air and yelled, "Holy Blueness!"

And Mom threw her hands up too and squeaked, "Beautiful!"

Which wasn't initially such a horrible series of events, but then all the hand flying caused the curry to fly through the air and land just above the hem of my dress.

Mom squealed at first, but then pulled herself together. "Let's get this mess cleaned up," she said in a calming voice.

I should've helped, but all I could do was stare at Ian.

He'd noticed the dress, but did he *notice* it? But then all I could do was notice *him*. He was wearing a black tuxedo, and it made him look powerful. Rugged, tall, and a bit lanky, too, but he looked so . . . manly. But then I glanced down and noticed he wasn't wearing dress shoes—he was wearing Converse high-tops. Turquoise.

His long brown hair flopped in his eyes as he looked down at his shoes. "I couldn't find the right shade of blue. I thought we could match. Sorry."

I leaned in and made him look up at me. "We match." My instinct was to reach out and gently tuck his hair behind his ear, but Mom was watching. Plus, we had a whole night ahead of us— there'd be plenty of time for playing with his hair.

Mom apologized over and over while she scrubbed the floor with lemon-smelling cleaner, which always made my nose itch. And

Ian just smiled as he scrubbed the bottom of my dress with a wet washcloth. I smiled back at him and scratched my nose.

He managed to get the chunky parts off, but the stain was forever. At the time, I didn't mind one bit. Ian Clark, with adorably floppy brown hair, was on his knees, washing my dress.

Butterflies.

If Mom hadn't been in the room, it would've been the perfect time to plant that first kiss on him. The Moment of Lip Lock Bliss. I had been deprived of lip lockage for eight months, twelve days. My whole body ached, starving for boy contact. But this kiss was going to be worth the wait.

Ian would hold my gaze, I imagined, then run his fingers through my wild, un-hair-sprayed hair and press his lips against mine. And I would know once and for all which category he belonged in.

But I was an excessive fantasizer; plus, I already had a perfect plan for The Moment of Lip Lock Bliss and it didn't involve my kitchen, yellow curry, and certainly not my mother.

Ian stood up and turned to my mom. "We're going to Dan's for a pre-party. I'll try to keep her away from anything liquid and yellow, Mrs. Griffith."

I took a breath. "My personal stain fighter." I may have even twirled my dress a little when I said it.

Mom pressed her lips together tightly, trying to control her quivering lip. "I wouldn't feel good about Justina going to prom with anyone but you." She reached out and dusted his tuxedo sleeve.

Just then, I felt a lick. Sol was doing his part to clean up my stain. I guess he really did like coriander. "Could you put him in the backyard, Mom? He's going to eat my dress."

"Sol, baby. Come here." She patted her hip as if she were giving a command, but she had already gone back over to the stove and was throwing more spices into the stew. Mom always called the dog "baby," and she rarely made him obey. She didn't want him to be *uncomfortable.*

Ian snapped his fingers. "Sit."

Sol stopped licking me. And he actually sat. Ian rubbed him behind the ears and told him he was a good boy.

"Wow," I said. "Persuasive." I wasn't sure if it was the finger snapping or the forcefulness in his voice or the rubbing of the ears, but I suddenly couldn't wait to get to the pre-party and away from Mom. Ian seemed to know exactly when to be gentle and when to put on the pressure. I had to know if this would translate into a perfect kissing technique.

A low grumble in my stomach interrupted my Ian daydream, reminding me of another reason I was eager to get to the pre-party: Dan's parents were preparing appetizers. I wasn't sure I could make it until dinner without a quick snack, because without proper food intake I start to make bad decisions.

In addition to the food and the kiss I was going to rock Ian's world with, I was also excited because Hailey was going to be there, my best friend—my best *girl* friend—and she was Dan's date. I liked him because he was the second nicest guy on the planet, and also because he had a pool and Hailey and I had an open invitation to swim whenever we wanted. Dan always got us whatever we wanted to eat and drink (orange soda and licorice, thank you), then he'd go inside to play video games and let us have our "girl time" by the pool. Fabulous.

But it felt like over the past year Hailey and I had detached from the hips and only saw each other on rare occasions— those seven minutes when our lunch periods overlapped, the occasional *Buffy the Vampire Slayer* marathon, and when it was warm enough to swim.

And I hadn't been to a party in months. Operation Lips Locked was in effect, and parties were like meth to a girl in love with kissing. So Hailey partied solo. Lately, since I carpooled to school with Ian, and she drove with Dan, most of our friendship was spent waving at each other from the passenger seats of other people's cars.

I missed her. But not just that . . . I hadn't even told her that my feelings for Ian had changed. I wasn't sure how she'd react. Would she be happy for me? Or feel left out?

"Here's your corsage." Ian pulled out flowers, but they weren't daisies.

Roses. Not white, for friendship. Not red, for love. They were roses that had been spray-painted glittery blue. The *exact* color of my dress.

"Blue roses?" I swallowed hard. What was he trying to say to me with blue roses? "For . . . patriotism?"

"No. Yes. I don't know." He pinned it on my dress, then leaned in and whispered in my ear, "Your mom said it had to be blue."

"My *mom* said?!" I suddenly realized that all this blueness—his shoes, the flowers, the blue purse and watch now laid out on the kitchen table—had been Mom's doing. I was an only child, true, but her need to be involved was approaching Creepsville. She didn't need to drape me in matchy-matchy "just like she wore" garb simply because I was her only living offspring. I wasn't a dress-up doll. Put a sweater on the dog and leave me out of it, for crying out loud.

I quickly pulled away, searching for a time machine portal—the only thing I figured that might save me—but that's when the corsage pin, which seemed to be the size of a samurai sword, jammed into my collarbone.

It took both my mom and Ian applying direct pressure for five minutes to get the bleeding to stop. But during that time, Mom explained it was true she had looked up his number on my cell and given him a quick call to explain the beauty of roses that matched a dress.

She actually said those words. *Beauty of roses that matched a dress.*

"Mom, it doesn't match the dress. It looks like it's *part* of the dress!" I lowered my voice and said, "This isn't your prom, Mom. It's mine."

She nodded, looking embarrassed. I felt bad for saying it.

"It's my fault. I can take it off." Ian reached out, and that's when I noticed his face had lost color. He looked mortified. Crap. Whenever Ian makes a mistake he always feels nauseous. One time just before a track meet, he realized he had worn the wrong color jersey, and he puked in the bushes.

Mom didn't need to call him and get involved. He didn't need to feel this way.

This ship needed to get turned around, quick. "I don't mind. I like it," I lied. The color slowly came back to Ian's face. Whew.

Mom went back to stirring her pot of curry. Under her breath she said, "I shouldn't have gotten involved."

I walked up behind her. "It's okay, Mom." But it wasn't.

"I won't call him again," she said as she blew on her spoon and tasted. "I'll delete his number from my phone. I shouldn't have it." When Mom felt forced into a corner she suddenly became the founder of the Melodramatic Moment of the Month Club. Time to pull her back out.

"You should have his number." I stood behind her, resting my chin on her shoulder and whispered, "For emergencies. Okay?"

She blinked repetitively, which meant she was thinking. She stirred. Blew. Tasted. Then said quietly, "Just for emergencies."

I grabbed Ian by the arm and told him we needed to go, that we didn't want to be late for the pre-party, and promised Mom, again, that I'd be home by two, and reminded her to put Sol in the backyard or else he'd pee on the carpet. Mom always chose his warmth and coziness over his bodily functions.

"But he'll get cold," she complained. "We'll both be gone for most of the night."

"Even if you come back by ten, he still needs to be able to pee, Mom. Leave him in the backyard. Lock the gate."

I couldn't believe Sol's well-being was always in my hands. And I couldn't believe we were having this discussion in front of Ian. Like he wanted to know these details.

My face flushed. I reached up and touched my cheek and realized what was happening . . . I was embarrassed! It didn't make sense. Talking about pee was making me embarrassed? Before tonight Ian had farted and burped in front of me countless times, and I may have done the same in an emergency moment here and there, but neither of us hardly even blinked.

Except we had now clearly moved past the Just Friends stage, because my face flushed when I discussed dog pee in front of him. Oh, lord. There was no going back.

"I worked at the dog pound one summer," Ian volunteered. "So be sure to lock the gate. I spent most of my summer chasing down lost dogs who got out because of a gust of wind."

"Now see"—Mom sunk her chin into her hand—"that is such a fulfilling job. Taking care of others." She was looking at me as if I were supposed to respond, *Yes, he's perfect. Let's gift wrap him.* But I already knew that. I didn't need her approval on this one.

I really couldn't stand and watch her dote on him anymore. Especially because I knew if she got any more comfortable, she might start in with her story about—

"Did I ever tell you I was elected prom queen?"

"Mom, no."

Ian's face lit up. "Oh, you *were*?"

I held my hand up. "Don't encourage her."

He ignored me and slid into a kitchen chair. "Go on."

Ian has this thing with listening to people's stories. He loves it when people talk about their past—it utterly fascinates him. Like if we are in a coffee shop, nine times out of ten he is able to strike up a conversation with a random stranger and get them to tell some bizarre story about how they once sat next to an NFL quarterback on a plane, or how they single-handedly got an entire room of stockbrokers to sing show tunes. The stuff he found out about people was always random.

When Mom started up with her "I was elected prom queen" story, Ian beamed like Rudolph on Christmas Eve.

And so Mom went on with her old, sad story about how she was chosen prom queen, but when she went up on stage she grabbed the microphone and made a public service announcement about the benefits of using public transportation and riding bikes, but this was the generation of the V-8 Trans Am with gold trim, so the only applause she got came from the chaperones.

Ian turned to me, smirking, which meant a setup. "What are you going to say in your acceptance speech tonight?"

I tilted my head and played right along. "My fellow students, as your prom queen, I declare that all future proms will be bonfires on the beach with veggie burritos."

He shook his head. "According to your definition, we had prom last weekend. And the weekend before that."

"Exactly. I'm a warm sweatshirt and bonfire kind of prom queen."

He looked me up and down, then raised an eyebrow. "Not tonight."

Toe-dip.

Mom cleared her throat. "You were nominated for prom queen, sweetheart?"

"I nominated her," Ian explained. "And so did Hailey, but Justina forced us to take her name off the ballot. And I mean *actual* force. Her nails are pointy. She broke skin, Mrs. Griffith."

Oh lord, he was cute.

But being prom queen was not an item I wanted to check off on my Things To Do Before I Die list. Queen of the Daisies? Queen of all Black Boots? Now that I could handle.

Even though deep down, deep in the dirty soles of my crusty boots, I secretly did want to wear that prom queen crown. Only because I wanted Ian and me to be the couple that slow danced together while everyone watched and swayed along and said longingly, "Oh my god, they are the cutest couple."

But the title of prom queen was always reserved for the most undeserving—whoever was enjoying the biggest scandal at the time would take the crown, it seemed. And I had my bet on Brianna or Allyson. Brianna had that recent champagne incident that ended up in an embarrassing viral video and Allyson was rude to *everyone*, so the prom queen bar wasn't raised very high at Huntington High.

So maybe I *would* make a good prom queen. But then again, if I did win, the entire school would be looking at me in this dress and these shoes. I glanced down at my outfit and suddenly became overwhelmed by my own blue-i-ness.

This may have been a very bad mistake.

I pushed the crazy talk out of my head—literally. . . . I pressed on my forehead with the palm of my hand to make the thoughts disappear. A technique that usually worked, but not always. And not in this instance. Dang it. But the night had already started— there was no do-over. Sometimes you just have to work with what you have. Thankfully I had watched enough *Project Runway* to know that.

I quickly snatched my purse and looped my arm through Ian's. "Let's go, Stainfighter."

We waved to Mom as we headed down the driveway. She stood watching us, still pressing her lips together tightly to stop the quiver. She didn't even notice Sol licking the spoon in her hand.

That's my dog. Badly behaved, but a resourceful little sucker. He's not just a dog to me, he's people. "Good boy, Sol."

Just before we got to the car, I turned to Ian. "You didn't *have* to get me a blue corsage just because my mom called. You could've said no."

"Like I'm going to say no to your mother. She's your mother. She's Peg Griffith! Phlebotomist of the Year!"

I shoved him. "Shut up, goof."

"I'm not saying no to Peg. Even though I wish I would've said no to that curry."

I smiled. "She was never going to give you a choice. Peg is eager."

Which was exactly why I looked like the Uni-Color- Bomber on my prom night.

"Can I talk now?" He was bouncing on his toes.

I folded my arms, preparing for what he was about to say, then nodded.

"Two things. One, we're going to dance to a Journey song tonight—I don't care how much you protest, I will dance you into submission—and second, I brought you a peanut butter cookie in case you get hungry and turn all old- man cranky on me."

This made me smile. I liked that he was prepared for my low-blood sugar moments. It made me happy with my decision to make this the night we would finally kiss.

"Oh wait," he added. "There's a third thing."

I looked up.

"The color." He gently lifted my skirt up high, but not *too* high, then let it fall back softly onto my thighs. "You look . . . nice."

Nice. Did he say *nice*?! What does that mean? Boring? Uninteresting? A dirt clod? A lentil?!

He must have sensed my ridiculous raging silent monologue, because he grabbed my hand, led me to the car, then leaned over and whispered in my ear, "You're not like any other girl, Justina. Thank God."

Oh my word, I have been kiss-deprived long enough.

It was time for me to put Ian in his correct kissing category. Most people wouldn't put this much forethought into a kiss, but I knew what it would mean for Ian and me. We wouldn't be friends anymore. And there would be no going back. But I was ready. Hopefully he was too. And I knew the exact moment and place I hoped it would happen.

Next to Dan's pool, in the far corner, was a hot tub. It was surrounded by ferns and sweet-smelling gardenias. It was lush. It was quiet—other than the sound of bubbling water, but water features are totally romantic. It was perfect. My plan was to take him out there to discuss something, maybe tell him a story about my childhood, like a good Christmas story because he always seemed to love those, then we'd stare at each other for an awkwardly long moment, but neither of us would look away, and then we'd step closer to each other, tilt our heads in opposite directions, and at precisely the right moment, our lips would touch, and *whammo*! I'd have my answer.

But, of course, that's not what happened.

I did manage to get out to that beautiful spot by the hot tub. And I stood next to the lush ferns and sweet-smelling gardenias.

And I got kissed.

But it wasn't by Ian.

Chapter Three

CORN DOG

"WAIT. YOU KISSED another guy?!" Gilda is poking at the hot dogs as they rotate on a greasy conveyor belt.

"Yes. No. Not intentionally." I readjust myself on the stool. "It's complicated."

Gilda closes the lid to the hot dog cooker, waits for the quiet click. "These things are."

I notice that she isn't offering me a hot dog; not that I'd eat one, but still. They are glistening—even the corn dogs have a thick warm glow about them, and I'm still starving.

The bell rings, and this lady wearing Bermuda shorts, a tank top, and a fanny pack attached tightly around her, well . . . fanny, flies through the door. "Morning, Gilda. Need my Red Bull. And my patch."

"Sure thing, Donna."

Donna heads off to search the refrigerators for her jumbo sugar-free Red Bull while Gilda digs through boxes next to the counter for a patch. A nicotine patch.

This feels like a routine these two have done many times before.

I can't help but stare at Donna. Her hair is transitioning to a light gray color, and it's so short it's spiky—almost dangerous looking, like a barbed-wire fence. She's strong, not like manly strong, but like garden-landscaping-rototilling strong. I say that because her nails are dirty, full of dark soil, or maybe pudding? And her arms are thick and tan, like a corn dog. I'm just so hungry!

Gilda starts ringing up Donna's order, and that's when Donna looks in my direction. She doesn't blink, doesn't pretend to be doing anything other than staring at me, and it's making me uncomfortable. "What happened to you, doll?" Her voice is strong and raspy.

I try to straighten out my dress, as if that will help. "I . . . I . . ."

"This poor girl got ditched. At prom," Gilda explains.

"Ditched? What kind of scumbag would do that to a sweet girl like you?" Donna peers over the counter to get a better look at me, and gives me the full up-and-down once- over. "Do your shoes match your dress?"

"Yes." I fiddle with my hem. "Mom's idea."

"Not a good one."

I look down, feeling the tears well up as I think about Mom and her eagerness to make me perfectly color coordinated—in *every* way. And how sick it makes me feel, given all the suffering I went through because of these stupid matching shoes. And now Donna, who I don't even know, is making me nervous with her dangerously spiky hair and eagerness to remind me of my bad decisions. "I really don't need to have the obvious pointed out right now," I say, like I'm all confident or something. But I can't even look her in the eyes.

"Aw, doll, listen up." She leans over the counter, folds her arms, and gets comfortable. "I got dumped once. Homecoming. Jessie Saxton took off in his van and left me stranded at the Ledbetter Community Center. I had to walk a mile to a Piggly Wiggly. It was humiliating. I know what you've been through." She pauses as if she's remembering the details. Her face grows tough, like jerky. "True, I kicked him in the shin for eyeballing another girl who it turns out was the girl in charge of playing music and he was giving her the eye to start playing our song, which was sweet and all, but still. How was I supposed to know?" She shakes her head, trying to convince herself. "No, he was going to be a scumbag *someday*. They all are."

Before she goes on, I say a quick silent prayer.

Please, please, Lord, don't let me grow up to be this hard and crusty. And forgive me for using the word 'crusty' but I couldn't think of anything else more descriptive.

But then I realize there may be some slivers of truth to what Donna's saying.

There's no excuse for what Ian did. I guess I should've known he'd turn into a scumbag *someday*.

I just wish that day hadn't been prom.

My stomach growls.

Donna looks over at the hot dogs and corn dogs rotating under the warm glow of fluorescent lights. "You want one? My treat."

"Don't you have a meeting?" Gilda starts bagging her box of nicotine patches. These two seem to know each other well. Maybe Gilda listens to stories from lots of her customers.

"There will be others." Donna winks and says to Gilda, "This young doll could use a corn dog. Don'tcha think?"

Gilda scuffles over to get me a corn dog, and I turn to Donna. "What kind of meeting?" I immediately realize it's probably an AA meeting and I should keep my mouth shut.

"DA meeting."

I crinkle my nose. "A what?"

"Debtors Anonymous." She pulls out a credit card and slides it across the counter. "I'm a compulsive spender. And a professional under-earner."

Gilda holds her hand up. "Forget it. Put that thing away. This one's on the house."

I might be the type of person to end up in DA one day too, but Mom's monitoring of my credit card keeps me in check. Most girls in my high school have credit cards, but they don't have spending limits like me, and they don't have moms who read their statements, making sure they only spend money at thrift stores, not the mall.

I have a $400 limit. Per *year*. That gives me $7.69 to spend on clothes every week. Since Tuesdays are orange-dot half-price at the Huntington thrift store, it's the only day I shop.

If I had my credit card with me right now, and it wasn't lost forever in the back of Brian Sontag's Prius, I'd use it to pay Gilda for the glistening corn dog. But all I can do is thank her. I smother the corn dog with ketchup, then hold it up and look at it. I haven't eaten meat in years. And I know how hot dogs are made. And I am disgusted that I'm about to break my pact to divorce myself from meat. But right now I'm so hungry I'd eat a bunny.

My hand trembles as I pull it closer to my mouth.

"It's a tofu dog," Gilda offers at the last possible moment. "I kinda figured you were one of those."

I cram the dog into my mouth. "Fank you!" I say, relieved that convenience stores have now become convenient for *my* type, too.

Donna leans over the counter. "So who exactly is this scumbag?"

"His name is Ian," Gilda answers for me, explaining where we are in the story since my mouth is full of tofu dog. "He picked her up for prom, he dazzled her mom and trained her dog and brought her a cookie, and basically presented himself as a perfect guy." She looks at me for permission, wondering if this is accurate. I nod and chew and swallow and she continues. "So they're on their way to some pre- party at Dan's house and Justina can't stop thinking about kissing him."

Donna nods, as if this story is familiar. "So you got tongue-tied with the guy in his car."

I shake my head and make out a somewhat audible, "No."

"Sucked face in the driveway?"

"No!"

"At the party?!"

Gilda sighs. "She never kissed him."

"Oh, no." Donna stands up straight.

"What?" I swallow hard and clear my throat so I can finally speak. "Isn't it a good thing I didn't kiss him?"

"No, doll. It's bad, real bad. You'll always wonder . . . was he or wasn't he?"

I know exactly what she is getting at. And she is absolutely right.

I can't believe I never got the chance to kiss you, Ian. Now that we're non-friends. A non-couple. A non . . . everything.

Donna folds her arms and lifts an eyebrow. "So why did Captain Scumbag ditch you?"

That's the zillion dollar question. I shake my head. "It's one of those long, complicated stories." My voice fades away.

"I hear you." Donna picks at the dirt under her fingernails. "I have some long, complicated stories. But it's not such a bad thing—it's because of those stories that I can proudly say I am the cougar I am today. Look it up—cougar—in the wiki encyclopedia."

"Wikipedia," I correct her.

She nods. "You've seen me, then."

I turn to Gilda, looking for answers. She holds her hand up like she can take it from here. "Justina's story isn't all that complicated. Not yet," Gilda explains. "All we know so far is Ian tried cleaning yellow curry off her dress and she thought it was adorable and she planned to kiss him at Dan's pre-party. She got a kiss, except it sounds like it was from someone else."

"Oh, you gotta tell me this story." Donna's eyes sparkle. She approaches me and reaches out to touch my blue dress, but pulls back. "What are these stains?"

I take a deep breath and settle onto my stool. Then I start to explain how the stains represent a tapestry of memories, and how they tell a story—

"That's all fine and good," Donna interrupts. "But let's get to Captain Scumbag. And more importantly, this other guy you kissed—scumbag number two."

"The kiss happened right after I got this." I point to a long black stain, the shape of a thin, wimpy corn dog, just above my knee.

Chapter Four
DIPPING SAUCE (SOY, I THINK)

WE PULLED INTO Dan's driveway, the diesel engine rumbling in Ian's old Mercedes—a clunky, distinctive sound that always made me feel comfortable. Most of the students at Huntington High drive cars that cost as much as a two- bedroom condo, and even though Ian's car is technically a Mercedes, the fact that the back window doesn't roll up and the seats have no springs and it is completely lacking in glamour makes me feel at ease. That car *is* Ian.

It was a long driveway—long enough to hold up to twelve cars, and we were lucky to snag the last spot. Dan lives in a neighborhood with sparkling sidewalks and manicured lawns—not a leaf out of place—and houses that have crisp American flags hanging *all* year round, not just on school holidays.

I live in a small cottage-type house with low ceilings and cracked countertops, over in the old part of town. When you drive down the streets around here, you'll be cruising in an immaculate suburban section, then sneeze and find yourself in a totally urban area. My house was zoned on the very edge of the Huntington High School district—I am one street away from being a Ledbetter girl.

Beautiful people streamed by us as we sat in Ian's car, waiting. For something. I wasn't sure what. Ian leaned over in his seat and tied and re-tied his turquoise Converse high-tops. His fear of tripping extended beyond the track.

"Double knot 'em, babe," I said.

"Babe?"

I was shocked it had come out of my mouth, too. But there it was—out there. So I had to go with it. "Yeah, it's a term of endearment." I narrowed my eyes, trying to look flirty—a look I had practiced hundreds of times by studying tampon ads in *Seventeen*. The girl always looks unhappy, but her crampy face also looks like her flirty face . . . pouty lips, narrowed eyes. "I endear you," I said.

He raised an eyebrow. My tampon-ad look must have worked, because he said, "I'll endear you later."

Toe-dip.

Maybe he was ready to take the plunge with me?

"Let's go." He popped a piece of Winterfresh gum in his mouth. But I couldn't move. I was an igloo—frozen and feeling a little hollow on the inside. Part of me—a *big* part—did not want to go through that front door. What was wrong with me? Why couldn't I do this?

When a limo pulled up to the curb, I had my answer.

A half dozen couples poured out of the backseat as the driver held the door open for them. They giggled as they stumbled by our car, clearly already tipsy. And the girls were looking a little too . . . *sophisticated.*

"Look at Brianna Portman's dress," I said, with my forehead pressed against the passenger window. "She looks like she's twenty-five years old. Come on! Does her slit really need to go *that* high up her thigh?"

"Maybe she has a ventilation deficit."

Before I could laugh, a puff of pink oozed by my window.

Eva Greer. His ex.

She was wearing a light pink dress with a full ball gown skirt that floated out from her hips like she was sitting in a rowboat. And she had a corsage with enough dark pink roses to enter as a float in the Pasadena Rose Parade. But even *she* knew not to match all her pinks.

I looked over at Ian and wrinkled my nose. "You okay?"

He pressed his lips together and paused. Then: "Yep."

Other than Eva, Ian had dated only one other girl, but that was in seventh grade and he dated her for like a year. Which by middle school standards was a world's record. Then he met Eva when we were freshmen. They were inseparable for two years before the Jimmy DeFranco Epic Party Disaster.

Ian is one of those Professional Boyfriends. He isn't a jerk who will do and say whatever it takes to get a girl to fall. And his full-of-swoon boyfriend acts sometimes make it into the lunchtime gossip report: He brought Eva a cup of ice to her table so her Diet Coke would be extra cold. He put cough drops in her locker when she complained of a scratchy throat. He looped pinkies with her when they walked down the hall.

Professional Boyfriend.

When he saw her kiss another guy, that was it. End of story. Some people have boundaries, or lines they just won't cross. That was his. I don't blame him.

I leaned over in my seat to catch Ian's eyes, giving him my not-sure-I-believe-what-you're-saying look.

"I'm fine," he said. "I'm over her. The girl thought we were meant to be together because both our names had three letters. She thought it was a sign from above."

I held back a laugh, but then we both gave each other a look and suddenly neither one of us could hold it in, and we laughed as we watched Eva trot up the driveway to Dan's party with her date—yep, Jimmy DeFranco. And it appeared Jimmy DeCheeseball had gone wild with the hair gel, because he was now sporting a faux-hawk.

I scooched my hand over closer to Ian, hoping he'd loop pinkies. But we weren't boyfriend/girlfriend yet. It wasn't in the nature of Professional Boyfriend to prematurely loop fingers. He knew exactly what he was doing, never leading anyone on until he was prepared to follow through.

And other than this prom night, he had only gone on one other date since he broke up with Eva. He won't admit to it being a date—more like "an agreement to do something"— but in my mind if that "something" involves a dinner, a dance, a midnight curfew, and premeditated showering . . . um, date.

Our friendship had been in full swing, and I hadn't seen him in that green shirt yet, so him going on a date didn't seem all that strange. At first.

It was three months ago, Sadie Hawkins dance—the one where the girls ask the guys. Allyson Moore—unafraid of anything, unfairly gorgeous, and sporting a chest that had popped out like two perfect tennis balls—bounced right up to Ian and asked him to go without even a flinch. I asked him why he said yes (like it wasn't obvious), and he said he couldn't say no. He just couldn't.

The night of the dance, I was curled up in bed in my jammies, my face covered in an apricot scrub mask, flipping channels aimlessly as I waited for him to call—to give me the full report.

"What are you doing?" he asked over the phone—it was pushing 11:45. At least he'd made curfew.

Flip, flip.

"Watching the College Bass Fishing Championship. That's cool, right?"

"And your definition of cool is . . ."

"What happened, goof?"

"She talked the whole night."

"And that's awful because . . ."

"She has a lot of thoughts about how to make flag corps better. A lot. Mostly having to do with shirt styles. I asked her about her family and within two sentences she was back to talking about the advantages of crops tops. Also, what is a crop top?" He laughed before I could answer, then blurted out, "But it's not like I minded looking at her lips all night."

Awkward. Awkward.

What was I supposed to say? I couldn't even push out an "Mmm-hmm" from my quivering lips. All I could do was wonder if Allyson spent the entire night looking at that crease.

He must have sensed the strange air that was billowing between us, because he immediately filled the awkward space with regular words. "But the food sucked and the band was okay, and I'm exhausted."

Exhausted? From looking at her lips? Her tennis balls?!

I don't know why I suddenly got jealous. It's not that I *wanted* him—not at that point, anyway—I guess I just didn't want to share him.

After that, he talked to her in the halls and did a lot of listening—just like him—but he never took it to the next level: no calls, no dates. I wasn't sure why. And I never asked.

Allyson must have given up, because a couple of weeks later the daily gossip report at lunch included news that she and Brian Sontag were now hooked up. No one even raised a brow at that—it was an obvious choice. They were of equal social standing—equal in hotness and equal in brain power—which on paper made them the perfect match. They quickly became an institution at Huntington High: there was Mr. Terry's undecipherable history notes, Friday night football games, and cute, cute Allyson & Brian—staples of the Huntington High experience!

Except that, as far as I could tell, Allyson and Brian were less of a couple and more like ice skating partners—moving around each other in a gorgeous, synchronized way, but never *really* touching each other.

"Everyone's heading inside." Ian tapped my knee. "Let's go."

I pressed the back of my head against the headrest as I watched limos appear outside Dan's house . . . Escalades, Hummers . . . and well-dressed, giddy people streamed by our car. Almost *all* of the girls looked like they were twenty-five, not just Brianna. And they were all done up like supermodels. Their shoes were strappy. They were silver. They were gold. They were *not* dyed blue.

"I can't go in there." I chewed at my lip. My breathing was shallow and fast like it gets on the climb up the Goliath roller coaster at Six Flags just before plummeting twenty-five stories. That type of breathing means I'm worried my stomach is going to fly out the top of my head. So it was weird I was feeling the same way sitting in that driveway. But their shoes . . . gold, silver, dainty, sweet. They weren't blue and chunky.

Oh, God.

"It's one thing to have an iridescent blue dress," I said, "but an entirely different thing to have shoes and nails and a purse and a corsage that match." I felt bad about bringing up the matchy-matchy mess I had gotten myself into. Especially since I'd worn all this for him; but the reality of the type of party I was about to step into now enveloped me. Usually I don't mind being the odd one who wears all-black everything. Different is comfortable for me. But I was having *unusual* feelings . . . like I just wanted to fit in and be like the rest of them. I turned to Ian and huffed a little. "I am a human blueberry."

Ian focused on the facts. "What is *iridescent?*"

I grabbed some fabric from my dress and swayed it around to show him what it did in the light.

"You don't look like a blueberry. Blueberries don't shimmer like that." He glanced to see if that made me laugh. It didn't. So he went with the direct approach. "You look gorgeous." We looked at each other for an unusually long time without words, blinking, staring, fantasizing—at least I was. Then he broke the moment. "And patriotic."

"Shut up."

"You know I'm kidding."

I did know he was kidding. And his jokes had me soaring on cloud nine, hopeful that there was a tenth. But the feeling quickly evaporated. . . . This was a crowd I did not want to be a part of. And by "crowd" that meant about ninety percent of my class. Huntington

High wasn't a huge school, so when there was a party, we *all* went. Minus the ten percent who were debate clubbers or math clubbers or impressive-on-a- résumé clubbers who studied excessively and felt that a good night's sleep was necessary for overachieving.

Which wasn't me, but it seemed that recently all I did on the weekends was hang out at the beach with Ian or watch *Buffy* marathons in my jammies with Hailey. So this scene was suddenly feeling out of my league.

In the past, I'd navigated plenty of parties, but Hailey had always been the lead. She orchestrated who to talk to and where to stand. I wasn't quite sure how to handle a scene like this without Hailey next to me preparing me for the entrance—the most important component to becoming a party warrior, according to Hailey. But Ian was a right- beside-me kind of guy. I had no one to follow, and I was out of practice.

"Have fun in there," I said, pretending to be upbeat. "I'm going to sit right here and supervise this front seat."

"Stop."

"I'm serious. I look like a piece of fruit. They're going to eat me alive like I'm Sunday brunch."

"Stop worrying about what people think about you." "They're going to mush me up and put me in a scone."

"Stop."

"I'm done. I'm pie."

"They don't care. They're thinking about their own mismatched socks. Look—" Ian pointed out the window.

Brian Sontag was standing by the front door lifting his pant leg. He was getting severely reprimanded by Allyson Moore for one sock being black and the other being clearly navy. She was using lots of hand expressions. He was shrugging a lot. Their evening had started off lecture-style. Not fun.

Ian poked me on the shoulder. "Do you think those two care about your choice in *shoe color*?"

I couldn't help but laugh. Ian always managed to turn my thinking around. Suddenly it hit me that I was going to prom with him. Ian Clark had asked *me*. Not Allyson. She probably didn't even know about the crease.

Maybe that's something he reserves only for me. God, I hope so.

I looked him over, admiring the one curl that was hanging over his eye, and decided to only focus on finding a way to get Ian Clark out back by the lush foliage. This boy needed to kiss me. Soon.

I touched his arm. "Let's go." "Wait." He held his hand up. "Sit right there." Ian jumped out of the car and took a few long strides (long strides were his specialty in the 4 by 100), and the next thing I knew he was opening the car door for me. I felt strangely…girly. And I liked it. There was never any doubt— whenever he was near me, I always felt better.

Dan's father answered the door. "Ian! Justina! Come on in!" Mr. Dunbar was very upbeat. He always wore a sweater vest.

As he led us to the kitchen, I waved at Dan's mother— she was in the living room sitting on the chaise lounge, reading a yoga magazine. She didn't say hello. Just smiled and nodded. Mrs. Dunbar is one of those serene uninvolved mothers. I secretly wished she was mine. Even if only for a day. Like *this* day. Then maybe I'd have taken the advice of a prom magazine editor and I'd be wearing a beautiful black strapless dress and silver shoes and a daisy corsage.

Ian guided me through the crowd, pressing his hand against the small of my back. I felt protected, like he was ready at a moment's notice to defend me against incoming missiles or flying swords or mall security. No one could get to me.

My face flushed and I wanted to belt out loud, "Look! Ian Clark is touching my back. My *back*. We aren't just friends anymore!" People had known us as *Just Friends!* all year. I wasn't sure if they would realize we were more. Or about to be.

Dan was standing in the middle of the kitchen, leaning over the huge granite counter island and organizing a tray of cheese and crackers. It was one of those kitchens big enough to hold Thanksgiving dinner guests *and* a game of football. There were zillions of people from our class crammed in the room shouting, laughing, eating.

Of course the surfer Mikes were there. Those two guys never missed a single party. Or a stellar shore breaking wave. You could barely tell them apart, both with their shaggy hair, worn T-shirts, untied shoelaces, and constant surf talk. The only discerning characteristic about them was the shade of their hair. One had very light blond hair, practically white like a cotton ball, and the other Mike had not-so-blond hair, but also not-so-brown hair, more like the shade of a city squirrel.

Most people referred to them as Mike and Other Mike. Their conversations were hard to follow. I should know—I was the third member of their chemistry lab group. They called me Sweetness. My guess was they gave me that nickname because they referred to every party as "sweet" and I was a party girl.

I don't think they noticed I hadn't been to many parties lately. They weren't ones for detail. But I was impressed that they had slicked back their hair and put on tuxedos. Sort of. Their ties were already undone. And now Mike was raiding the refrigerator while Other Mike was leaning against the counter eating rolled-up bologna.

This made me hungry, even though I knew how bologna was *really* made. But I decided I would hold off on eating so my breath would be ready for my moment with Ian out back by the gardenia bush.

Hailey pushed her way through the crowd and hugged me. "You look gorgeous!"

"Thanks." I tried not to look down at my feet. Didn't want to bring attention there.

Ian leaned in. "She thinks she looks like a turnip."

"I'm a blueberry."

"No, the color is perfect," Hailey said. "Makes your eyes sparkle."

That's what best friends are for. Finding what sparkles when you're in the middle of a disaster.

I suddenly wished I had taken her up on her offer for us to get ready together. Maybe she would've given me a heads-up about choice in shoes and maybe she would've convinced me to wear all black. I could've looked gorgeous tonight—not like a piece of tough-skinned fruit. I suddenly wanted to turn around and go join Mrs. Dunbar on the couch. I wanted to be *uninvolved*.

I looked Hailey over, trying not to reveal my I-wish-I- wasn't-this-jealous face. "You look . . . amazing." I wasn't exaggerating at all. Her dress was exactly what I would've chosen . . . a straight black strapless full-length gown. Gorgeous. And of course she was wearing silver heels. When I took a closer look at her, she looked twenty-five, like everyone else. "Wait. Are you wearing falsies?"

Hailey batted her lashes. "Glam, aren't they?"

She did look glam. I was surprised she'd done something so drastic without warning me first. But then again, this was Hailey—the girl who did what she wanted, and when she got caught, talked her way out of it. Hailey knew exactly how to turn the tables. *Roll and deflect.* That was her motto. She was an emotional escape artist. Which she'd learned from her dad—he had a black belt in jujitsu and always used martial arts techniques as metaphors for life. For Hailey, it worked. Sometimes I just wished I knew how to kick someone in the shins. All my dad had ever taught me was No Means *No*. But it doesn't work on dogs (or humans) without the assertive part. Hailey had assertive juice coursing through her veins.

"What's with all the skin tonight?" Hailey eyed some girls near us. "And what's up with the slit in Brianna's dress? It goes all the way up to her hoo-hoo."

I laughed. "I heard she has a ventilation deficit."

"Yeah, well a slit like that isn't doing much for that stellar reputation of hers."

I turned to her. "Not that ours are much better."

"We're the good girls," she said as she looped her arm in mine. "We just like to have fun."

That's my Hailey. She has a reputation for being a wild one, but she knows how to spin it. . . . *I'm the fun one!* This helped her popularity, luckily, because everyone seemed to respect her upbeat, I-don't-give-a-crap-what-you- think attitude. Or maybe they were scared of her?

Either way, being best friends with her made me quietly popular. Except my bad-girl reputation didn't earn me tons of respect—it earned me silent glares. Fortunately, it didn't result in all-out nastiness. Not often.

That's because Hailey's friendship provided me with a sort of invisible social protection—you mess with me, you get her.

The entity that was known as Hailey & Justina (inseparable, unstoppable) had started in ninth grade. Neither of us had been looking for a boyfriend, of course, because we were too swept up in the massive selection of high school guys. Middle school had been like shopping for dinner at a gas station—not much selection. High school was like the smorgasbord at the Hometown Buffet. So we'd hit every party we could, which hadn't been hard since Hailey had the confidence of a party ninja. She just walked in as if parties were her invention, and I followed.

We'd pick out adorable guys who looked kissable and make it a sporting event—calling them like a game of pool: eight ball, corner pocket. Except it was, "Sandy blond, next to the chips." We were highly successful . . . mostly due to Hailey's revisions of my all-black-everything look. I still wore all black, but she'd taught me to buy formfitting sweaters, not button- down shirts, and to use a pop of color, but only on the lips. It draws their eyes in, and lips are the only part of your body you want guys to focus on, she'd say.

That and boobs, which Hailey had also revised for me after a quick visit to Victoria's Secret. I wasn't sure I even needed a bra due to my less-than- impressive size. But her philosophy was that all girls could have cleavage thanks to the invention of the Miracle Bra. No excuses for not having lady lumps, she'd say.

After the introduction of the Miracle Bra to my wardrobe, my kissing stats increased threefold.

All through tenth grade we were still in the game. Only, by the end of the year, I was getting tired of referring to guys by hair color and room position and not by their actual names, and I was looking for the real thing. Except after the events at Jimmy DeFranco's party that summer, we were no longer being referred to as The Girls At That Party. We had a reputation.

Which had never been my intention—it had started out as a hobby, really. Oh god, that sounds gross, but kissing boys was simply a highly enjoyable activity. I'd never thought about the consequences . . . hallway glares from girls, hallway winks from guys, and oh-so-rude remarks from Brianna Portman, which were never limited to just the hallways. I wish she'd just stuck with glares, like the rest of them.

So now I couldn't even make a move without weighing the consequences of each step. But it seemed to me that eight months and twelve days without kissing a single boy had been long enough to erase the damage.

But I wasn't so sure.

Ian squeezed my elbow. "Gonna go talk to Dan."

I nodded. From behind, Ian looked like a grown man. Except his hair had flopped over to the wrong side but in one of those cute ways, which made him one hot burrito.

"Wow. Stare much?" Hailey was sucking on green Jell-O. "If I didn't know better, I'd say you two have moved past the friendship phase."

My face flushed. I bit my lip. Her eyes grew big. "No. Way."

"We haven't done anything about it. But we are tonight."

I couldn't believe the words came out. I shut my eyes tight and braced for impact.

"This is *so* like you to not tell me. I can't believe this. I'm so mad!" Hailey wrapped her arms around me and bear- hugged me. "And so happy!"

My body relaxed in her arms. She was happy. Whew. For some reason I felt like something official had just happened. Like we'd passed through an invisible barrier. Because, when it came to Hailey, I had this problem with assuming nothing would ever change. And if it did, it would hurt. But at this moment it wasn't hurting at all.

We unwrapped our arms, and I noticed her eyes were wet. Her falsies were glistening.

"He doesn't know yet," I said.

"What?"

"I haven't exactly told him. See, he wore this green shirt to my house a few weeks ago and—"

Hailey put her hand up. "Sweetheart, have you gone crazy crackers? Aren't you worried this will mess up your friendship?" She wasn't one to get tied up with shirt color details. And crazy crackers was what she always called me when I waded a little too far into the deep end.

"Ruining our friendship is *all* I worry about. Believe me."

She put her hands on my shoulders. "It's okay. He's gonna fall for you. I don't know when, but it'll happen for you guys."

I crinkled my nose. "Actually, we're going to kiss." I leaned in and lowered my voice. "I mean, I hope we are. In just a few minutes."

"You know *when*?"

I nod. "And where."

"Why is this not surprising? You're my little daydreamer." She dabbed at her eyes with her knuckles: then, when she was sure of dryness, she raised an eyebrow. "All right . . . where?"

I don't tell her that I originally imagined us kissing at night under an umbrella with the stars falling around us because that would sound insane. "Out back. By the hot tub."

"By the ferns and the gardenias. Oh, totally." She reached into her purse, which was silver and beaded. So glam. "Altoid. Very strong. Here."

I popped the mint in my mouth. My eyes watered a little. "What about you and Dan? Any love connection there?"

"We've talked about it. But we're just staying friends." She seemed a little disappointed.

"Is that . . . okay?" I asked, trying to hold back my tears, but these were caused by the curiously strong mint.

"It was my decision. I think he'd definitely give it a whirl if I let him. But I told him it wasn't going to happen. Probably hurt the guy's feelings." She looked across the room at Dan. "Except now I don't know."

"Don't know what?"

"If it's this yummy green Jell-O or the fluorescent kitchen lighting, but . . . I think I'm attracted to him."

I squealed. "That's great!" I was so happy to hear that. It made me feel relieved to think of Hailey finding someone who was boyfriend material, too. She and Dan are ideal for each other. Dan is the star left wing on his soccer team. Hailey is right wing. Having opposite strong sides would make a perfect balance.

Plus, Dan was the one who had taught Hailey how to drive. Her mom had overused the phrase "next week, I promise," so Dan took her to the Target parking lot in his dad's Jag and showed her all she needed to know. Which meant he was patient and reliable.

"Ladies!" Dan and Ian had made their way back over to us. "We're doing dessert first tonight." Dan presented us with a couple of Jell-O shots.

Hailey waved him off. "No more for me. One was enough."

"I've already had five, but that's your call, Miss Hailey." Dan winked at her.

She smiled and said, "Maybe Justina wants one."

Dan handed me a small plate with a cube of cherry Jell-O. "Don't have any blueberry. Sorry, Justina."

I smirked and looked over at Ian. He nodded at me. "Of course I made him say it."

I took the Jell-O and held it up. "Cheers! Here's to Dan and Ian. The two most respectable guys we know!"

"No, tonight I'm Dan-O the Man-O!" He gave a wicked laugh. Oh lord, this was going to be an interesting night. The guys slurped theirs down, but I held on to mine.

Hailey was right about making sure I was ready for that kiss. The Altoid had left a fresh taste I didn't want to ruin.

"Let's walk around." Ian dropped his plate in the sink and led us all out of the kitchen. Just as we got to the door, I realized I was still holding mine, so I quickly went back to get rid of it. And that's when I heard it.

"Nice shoes."

I turned around. My vision filled with perky tennis balls. Allyson Moore. She looked like a Grecian goddess in a stark white dress with a tight halter top and a skirt dripping with layers of chiffon. Her caramel-colored hair extensions were pulled back in a severe ponytail, which made her head look like a perfectly polished stone.

I couldn't bare to let my eyes drift down to her shoes. I knew they'd be gorgeous. But I couldn't help myself. I looked. Peeking out from the edge of her gown was a pair of strappy, silver shoes. They were heavenly—princess-grade. Allyson Moore was sleek, smooth, and regal—like a Great Dane.

Brianna pranced up, joining Allyson, her slit shifting and almost revealing her hoo-hoo. I couldn't help but quickly notice her shoes, too. Dainty, silver, strappy, and beautiful. And exactly the same as Allyson's. Their heels clicked and tapped lightly on the tile floor, sounding like percussion instruments.

My shoes were cinder blocks. *Thunk, thunk.*

I looked back up at them, unable to respond. What was I supposed to say? Thanks? Because clearly Allyson was being sarcastic since my shoes looked like navy vessels compared to theirs. I couldn't even understand why they were talking to me.

The only language Brianna spoke was sarcasm. In fact, she was fluent. And she was teaching Allyson well.

Allyson knew me because I was Ian's best friend, so she would wave at me ever so slightly when she was practicing on the field and I was running on the track. I don't think she even remembered we'd been friends back in fourth grade and she'd invited me to her birthday party. But that was back when friendships had been determined pretty much by seating assignments.

Now that we were in high school, our paths rarely crossed because I was always running and she was captain of the Huntington High School flag corps. Flag *twirlers*, as everyone liked to call them.

But twirling was not considered cool until Allyson Moore joined the team. They were just members of the marching band. But when she came along, she'd changed the uniforms to low-rise hot pants and crop tops. Suddenly the whole school wanted to go to the games to see them twirl. She was really dedicated to tightness-of-shirt detail.

"Wait, did you get those *dyed?*" Brianna said as she looped her arm through Allyson's. Then she wrinkled her nose like she'd just sniffed a jar of rubber cement. Unfortunately, the tone of her voice went up so high when she asked the question that it summoned all the other girls in the room to turn around and look at me. Some of them I knew. Katie from pre-calculus. April from history. Rose from drama. Suzette from detention (which I only got once because of excessive tardies—Ian and I sometimes listened to music in the parking lot a little *too* long). They all stared, waiting to find out my answer to Brianna's question.

These were not supportive stares. And this was beginning to feel familiar. But none of these girls at this party knew the truth of what had happened at Jimmy DeFranco's party. Only what was dished out over lunch when school started.

They glared at me as I pressed myself against Dan's sink, just like they'd been glaring at me since Hailey and I'd started our kissing game. But as I looked around, a few of their looks weren't the unsupportive kind—they were the feeling- sorry-for-me kind. Which thankfully made me feel like a human—not merely a lunch-time topic.

I decided the best approach was a direct one. Answer her question honestly and keep good posture. "Yes," I said, as I pulled my shoulders back. "I *dyed* them."

Allyson tilted her head. Brianna laughed and said, "So you thought the prom theme was an Easter egg hunt?" Which I'm sure she said for Allyson's enjoyment, since Allyson was the head of the prom planning committee. And that meant Allyson took all of this way too seriously.

I wished Hailey was standing there with me. She'd roll and deflect and make these girls run away crying about their own shoes. I wanted to confront them—tell them they were rude and stuck-up. But no, I ended up babbling on with details of my Highly Involved Mother Horror Story and how it was her idea for me to wear match-ing shoes, trying to get their sympathy, I guess.

Brianna stared at me blankly. "Um, gasp?"

Everyone laughed. Time to get even more direct. "At least they match my *dress*. Not another person."

I looked straight at their matching feet. Allyson stepped back, probably shocked at my direct comment. Even *I* was shocked by my direct comment. "They're Jimmy Choos," she said.

"They're not even yours?" I tried to play dumb.

Brianna tightened her lips. "No. That's the designer." She lifted her dress to make sure I could see them in their entirety. "These are four hundred and fifty dollar shoes."

I had no comeback. I was talking to girls who were wearing shoes that cost as much as a luxury car payment. I desperately needed Ian. He was always quick with the witty replies. But he was nowhere in the vicinity.

Allyson squinted at me. "Who are you looking for?"

Direct. Keep being direct. Don't back down. This will all be over soon, and you can move on to the kissing portion of the night. "I'm trying to find Ian."

The vision of Ian and Allyson at the Sadie Hawkins Dance popped into my head, and all I could do was stare at her lips. The ones he said he'd stared at the whole night.

Allyson perked up. "Ian. Ian *Clark*?"

"Yeah, he's my—"

"Where is he?" Allyson turned to Brianna. "I *have* to talk to him."

My voice cracked. "But we're—" It was too late. Allyson waltzed out of the kitchen in pursuit of Ian. Brianna stepped up to me. "By the way . . . *love* the matching rose."

She spoke sarcasm with an accent of evil.

But I had a sense of sarcasm too. Not highly developed, but it was there. I touched a petal on my corsage and said. "Thanks. I hope the Easter Bunny likes it." She had a confused look on her face when I pushed past her.

Why was Allyson suddenly looking for Ian? Of all the guys she could go for, why *him*? He'd turned her down. It was over. Well, maybe he didn't reject her, but it's not like he *pursued* her. That's practically the same thing! What was she doing?! I sped up and trailed behind her on her way out to the pool. But just as I got close, my cruise-ship-size foot got caught on the hem of my dress. I tripped and landed in a bed of pansies. Looking up, I saw Allyson still charging ahead— headed right for Ian. She didn't even notice me on the ground in a pitiful heap.

"Dude, what the—?" Other Mike helped me up off the ground. Then Mike swooped in on the other side and guided me by my elbow. "No more walking solo for you, Sweetness. These are danger-ous times, and you need shelter."

He was so obscure. But totally helpful.

As soon as I made my way out of the pansy bed, I turned to the Mikes. "Thanks, guys. I can walk a straight line now. My coordina-tion is back. I'll be sure to, you know, seek shelter."

"Solid." The Mikes gave each other a high five, like they were proud of their duo rescue effort. And that's when two girls came running outside toward us.

"Ladies!" Mike twirled, showing off his surprisingly good bal-ance. The girls squealed and hugged them. It was cute.

But they weren't Huntington High girls—they were Ledbetter girls. Both of them were wearing black-and-white dresses, almost matching but not quite, each with different animal prints. Cheetah? Snow leopard? And both of their gowns were backless. *Completely* backless. One wrong move and someone could have a viral video on the Internet. They both looked me over—they were up-and-down not-so-friendly looks. Or I don't-know-what-kind-of-looks, but I didn't want to stick around to find out so I quickly moved on.

The pool was the shape of a kidney, and beautiful people were wrapped around its edge. I turned and sucked in my belly, squeez-ing past well-dressed bodies, maneuvering my way out to the hot tub area.

Hailey was on the far side of the pool with Dan getting warm by an outdoor heater, so I walked on by myself and scoped out the hot tub. I wanted to get a good feeling for where I might stand when I planted it on him. Facing the house? The back fence?

As I moved around, I spotted Ian. He was on the far side of the pool talking to Allyson next to a potted palm. Talking to Allyson?

Next to a potted palm? I was not about to walk over to that side of the pool and engage in Moment of Lip Lock Bliss next to a *potted palm.*

Allyson was waving her arms around, talking in a frenzy, and Ian was inching away from her little by little. I could tell he was trying to get out of the conversation, but he was also the nicest guy on the planet. If someone wanted to talk to him, he was all ears.

But why was I suddenly feeling so lightheaded? Was this jealousy?

My stomach growled at me.

Oh. Maybe that's what this was about—low blood sugar. I was just being irrational because I was snack-deprived.

I took in a deep breath, let it out, and gave my growling stomach a pep talk about being patient, then got back to planning for The Moment of Lip Lock Bliss.

I paced back and forth, and when I found the right spot, I realized I was able to see everyone—Ian, Allyson, Hailey, (not Dan—he must've wandered off), and that meant they could all see *me.* This private spot was not going to allow for a private kiss with Ian.

But maybe I wanted it to be a little public. Maybe when Allyson saw me plant one on Ian, she'd go tell her stories to her *own* boyfriend—not mine. Or soon to be mine. Or whatever was about to happen.

"Green Jell-O?" Dan approached carrying a full tray.

"No. But you're buzzed. Maybe you should take it easy. Hailey will want you to remember this night." I motioned toward her. "Doesn't she look gorgeous?"

"Yeah. I guess." He shrugged without even looking her way. "The eyelashes are freaking me out, though. She looks like a spider."

"Dan!"

He laughed and almost fell over, but caught himself just in time so he wouldn't spill the Jell-O.

"Don't you feel kind of...you know...like maybe you should take your friendship to the next level?" I asked, trying to be leading. And probably sounding obvious.

"Not gonna happen." He was slurring his words. "We'll just have to settle for carpool buddies."

It hit me that he was acting like this because Hailey had turned him down. He probably felt he had to pretend it didn't bother him. I almost wanted to reach out and give him a hug—I felt sorry for him. Because I knew if Ian turned me down in the next few minutes, I couldn't say I wouldn't do the same thing.

He put his hand on my shoulder, mostly to help him steady his balance, but also so he could make his point very clear. "Look, I need your help."

"With?"

"Making someone jealous."

"Hailey doesn't get jealous. She's too awesome for that."

"Not her. Allyson Moore."

"You're confusing me."

"Girls only want what they can't have. If Allyson thinks you're after me, she'll want me."

"No. You're wrong. That's not how these things work. Girls like guys who—"

"Nah, they want a reason to get jealous. It's all like biological. Their DNA has a jealousy strand, or something."

I shook my head even though I wasn't entirely sure he was wrong. "But you're here with Hailey. Who is standing over there watching us, by the way. And I'm here with Ian."

"But everybody knows Hailey and I are just friends. There's nothing that would make Allyson jealous. But if *you* kiss me, her jealousy strands will act up. She's sooo hot! Will you just let me give you a kiss? No tongue, just lip." He sighed, looking impatient. "Or maybe a little tongue to make it authentic?"

"What? No!" I threw my hands back, not realizing that at that very moment Dan's father was walking by with a tray of sushi and dumplings with extra dipping sauce.

The bowl of soy sauce crashed to the ground and splattered on my dress, just above my knee.

"I'm so sorry, Justina!" His dad set the tray down.

"It's okay, Dad. I'll help her clean it off." Dan covered his mouth when he talked, clearly attempting to block his vodka breath. His dad smiled, picked up the tray, and walked on, probably enjoying the role of Gracious Host In Sweater, but not wanting to be involved in the messy parts.

So once again, I had a guy on his knees rubbing a spot off my dress. But Dan wasn't doing a very good job—he kept looking around. And clearly not for Hailey.

Dan was so buzzed he could barely focus on the stain— he kept scrubbing my kneecap with his sleeve.

"Forget it," I said. "The stupid dress is already ruined."

Dan stood up to face me. "Please. Just kiss me."

"So Allyson can watch? That is creepy!"

"She's right over there talking to Ian. It's perfect. We'll get 'em both jealous."

I popped up on my toes to get a glimpse of Allyson— just like I had at her fourth grade birthday party, only now she wasn't unwrapping the gift that she never thanked me for. . . . She seemed to be unwrapping Ian.

Allyson was *still* telling some story, and now Ian had cupped his chin with his hand and was nodding along with every word. Fascinating stories were like a drug to him. He wasn't inching away anymore. Was it possible Allyson Moore, flag twirler, could be *that* interesting?

Dan was right. Him kissing me would send Ian into a frenzy. It would send Allyson into a frenzy. But most of all, it would make Hailey mad. Which was why I'd never kiss Dan.

I shook my head. "No, Dan. It's not right. I won't—"

But it was too late. Dan planted one on me. The good thing was it was close-mouthed, and it technically didn't feel like an actual kiss because he rammed his lips on mine—it was more like a fender bender where two cars plow into each other and then there's swearing.

I kept my eyes open during the wreck of a moment and in the distance I could see Hailey. Looking right at us.

I turned my head away. "Stop it. Stay away from me!"

But Dan just smiled. "Hailey's not gonna mind. Watch."

Dan wobbled at first, then staggered over to Hailey and put his arm around her. He whispered something in her ear. But she shook her head, shoved him away and walked off. Which was exactly what *I* should've done.

Oh no. No, no, no. I couldn't hurt Hailey like this. This was not in the plan.

Ian kept nodding his head because of his enthralling conversation with Allyson. I wasn't sure if he saw the kiss. But if there was one thing I could do that would ruin everything between us, it would be to kiss another guy. At a party. A *pool* party! What was wrong with me?

I considered throwing myself into the pool. Was it deep enough to kill me *and* this dress? Mom would be so disappointed. But instead, I slumped into a lawn chair, aching for my Moment of Lip Lock Bliss, and waited to see if Ian would join me by the hot tub.

He didn't.

Chapter Five
A SLURPEE, JUMBO-SIZE, BERRY

"SO WAS THIS Dan at least kind of cute?" Donna raises an eyebrow.

Gilda gives her this let-her-tell-the-story, butt-out kind of look.

"Dan was not himself, that's for sure," I explain. "But it gets worse. It gets confusing. Ian is such a great guy . . . but then there's the daisy ring incident and the dress malfunction and the note from Eva. . . ." I sigh, realizing I'm getting ahead of myself.

Gilda fiddles with her braid. "Oh, no. His ex?"

I nod. "I don't know what to think."

Donna clears her throat. "Here's your problem, doll—you don't see the world as black or white, and you should."

"But it isn't black or white."

"So you're admitting you have a problem."

"There are grays," I say. "Things that aren't just yes or no."

"Aha! The problem." Donna rubs her hands together, proud of herself. Oh, sheesh. Maybe I do have a problem. I start to think about all the things Ian has done for me—brought me magazines when I was home sick, ordered me veggie pizza on his mom's credit card, teetered on the edge of flirtation with me.

But then there's Allyson. And Eva. His jealousy. Or lack of jealousy. Or whatever it was—I had no idea. "No. There are grays. The stuff in between." I shake my head. "The stuff I can't figure out. If that's a problem, then yeah, I have one."

"Let me tell you a little something about Donna Kramer."

I scratch at my hand—I always get itchy when people refer to themselves in third person.

She widens her stance, like a football coach. "First of all, I don't *see* the world, I stare it down like a lion does a helpless baby antelope. I wait and watch and pounce when I need to. Ya gotta stare the world down, doll. And by world, I mean *men*. You know that, right?"

I start to give her an answer, but she doesn't really want one.

"See, you gotta figure 'em out. Study them." Donna paces the floor in front of the counter. "Question them. Fill in the blanks. Make assumptions. Otherwise, you're left in a ditch on the side of the road on your prom night wondering why did this happen? And you never saw it coming. Am I right?" She doesn't wait for an answer. "Believe me, doll. Men are scumbags until they prove they're women."

My mouth drops. She's left me dizzy. But I know I've mastered one of her suggestions . . . question them.

Why did the night end like this, Ian? Did I really deserve to be ditched?

The bell rings and the sliding glass door opens. A tall, slim man wearing a well-fitting blazer and crisp khakis walks in at a brisk pace.

"Morning, Pastor Rick," Gilda says as she reaches to the front of the counter.

He nods to her, revealing his receding hairline, and heads to the bathroom.

"It's his Sunday morning routine," Gilda whispers as she places three items on the counter. A Twinkie, a bag of Pop Rocks, and a *National Enquirer*. "He says it pumps him up before his sermons."

Donna inspects the bag of Pop Rocks and reads the words out loud. "'Popping candy . . . for a kick!'" She nods. "I like this guy."

Pastor Rick soon joins us, his hands damp and clean, and gives friendly hellos and good mornings to all of us.

As Gilda rings him up, Donna bounces on her toes, clearly holding in something. I steady myself for the bizarre comment or question she's about to unload.

"Pastor, I just gotta know . . ."

Oh, no. Here it comes.

"Did God make men scumbags, or did they just figure that one out all by themselves?"

Pastor Rick doesn't flinch. Doesn't even blink an eye. He turns to her and plainly says, "A man's behavior is often a reflection of the way he's been treated by a woman."

Donna gives him a blank look. He sticks his hand out and shakes hers. "Have a lovely day." Pastor Rick leaves quietly, his feet not making a sound. His words zing around in my head: *the way he's been treated by a woman . . .*

I look down at my hand, the one that should be wearing the ring Ian gave me. I can't believe I made him take it back.

Crap. Is that what this is about?

"I know what will cheer you up." Gilda fills up a jumbo- size cup with berry Slurpee and sets it on the counter for me.

Donna is still staring at the door. "Pastor Rick," she says, under her breath. I'm not all that convinced she's the cougar she says she is.

"Do you think he's right? Guys behave the way they do because of the way we treat them?" I swallow my Slurpee hard, and feel the wave of a brain-freeze coming on.

Gilda shrugs, then connects looks with me. "Why? Because Dan forced a kiss on you? That wasn't your fault."

I press on my forehead, trying to push back the freezing pain. "There's more. I may have done something else. Maybe some of this *was* my fault."

Donna shakes her head. "No. You're the one who ended up in a ditch. It's black or white. No grays, doll."

"But there's this." I point to the next stain of the night—a greasy one just under my armpit. It has spread deeper into the fabric, looking like the shape of Alaska. "Ian said it was an accident." My eyes sting, and I can feel the tears gaining momentum again. "But now I'm not so sure."

Chapter Six

BUTTER

I DECIDED THAT going inside Dan's house and hiding in the bathroom was the best alternative at that point. Ian was probably off talking to Dan's parents, thanking them for a lovely time, completely oblivious to the fact that their son had just rammed his lips into mine. Ian was always comfortable with *other* people's parents, maybe because his mom and dad were . . . confusing.

His parents were the divorced kind that probably never should have divorced. I'd never seen exes nicer to each other than his parents: high fives, compliments, birthday gifts, apologies. Ian doesn't even have a memory of their marriage being bad—just memories of their divorce being good.

Comforting, but still . . . confusing.

I think that's why he's always been the Perfect Boyfriend. He never wanted to be the one who gave up too soon.

I lingered in the bathroom, scared to face Hailey. She was going to lose it. What would she do? I kissed her prom date. Right in front of her!

After giving myself a pep talk in the bathroom mirror (one of those where you convince yourself there's some sort of silver lining in every situation, even though you know you're lying to yourself), I finally decided to go back out and face what I had done.

I carefully walked down the hall, trying to dodge the sculptures of glass dolphins, and as I rounded the corner, I suddenly found myself nose-to-nose with Hailey.

"It's not what it looked like." I reached for her hand, and luckily she let me take it.

"Forget it. Dan's a jerk." She looked off with a vacant stare. "He's not interested in me."

"He's drunk."

"I know. I can't even get a *drunk* jerk to like me?" Hailey paused, leaning against the wall. "I've always been able to get any guy I wanted. So why can't I get Dan? He likes me—I don't like him—I like him—he kisses you. What's wrong with *me*?"

"It's not you. It's timing. I guess you both needed to want each other at the exact same moment."

She rubbed her temples. "Good lord, love is impossible. I mean, how do people ever even find each other?"

I shrugged. She was right—it did seem impossible. What were the odds that Ian and I were going to feel the same way about each other at the same precise moment? What if we leapfrogged each other forever, never landing together in the same spot?

Hailey forced a smile and stood up straight. "So we'll go to prom as friends. At least I'll get to drive his dad's Jag since Dan's too drunk. It has an amazing sound system."

That's my Hailey. Finding sparkle in a disaster.

I gave her my big-eyed hopeful look. "So . . . do you wanna..."

"Of course I do."

And we did. We hugged it out.

Ian peeked his head around the corner. "You two ready?"

My stomach free-falled. I had no idea if he'd seen me get kissed, and I wasn't ready to deal with it. Watching Hailey and Dan lose out on a relationship because of timing was unbearable—and it felt like I was going to lose out on a relationship because of *Dan's* timing. The jerk.

The car ride to the hotel was not ideal—it was silent. I counted trees and streetlights to occupy the time, but when I got to my eighteenth oak, I decided the uncomfortable silence lounging in the front seat needed to be shoved out the window.

I took the not-at-all direct approach. "Allyson Moore is rude."

"Justina."

"She was trying to make a move on you."

"She needed a favor." He gripped the steering wheel tightly. "She's head of the prom committee, and she wanted me to help move decorations."

"You don't need to do favors for that girl. You can say no." I hated to be the mothering type, but sometimes he needed to have things explained clearly.

He let out a big sigh. "Give her a chance. She can be a good friend."

"Friend? She knew we were there together, and she was trying to figure out a way to get you to listen to her sad, dumb flag-twirling stuff."

"Prom committee stuff."

"Even worse," I said, looking down at my dress and realizing I was bunching up the fabric inside my fist. "Why can't she get her own boyfriend to help her?" I breathed in and let the air out slowly, making sure my words came out smooth and calm. "You don't even have to answer. . . . It's because she wants *you*, Ian, that's why."

He immediately shook his head, not even taking a moment to consider this might be true. "You always assume the worst."

"No. I try to figure people out before they screw me over."

"Which keeps you from doing what you really want to do."

"What are you talking about?"

"The daisy ring."

Oh no. I could not believe he was bringing up the daisy ring incident now. "Why are you bringing this up now?"

"Because you, Miss Justina, have an assumption problem. The first step is admitting it."

"Okay. Fine. I admit it—I assumed the worst. But we've been over this, Ian. I even formally apologized. You forced me to, remember?"

A few weeks ago, Ian bought me a gift. It was a ring. With a daisy on it. Normally, that would be cute and appropriate and endearing, but the daisy was big. *Huge.* It was the width of two fingers! The ring was actually hugely awesome, but something like that screamed, *Look at my ring, it's ridiculously huge and you should make fun of me! Glare even more at me!* I had spent the last eight months trying not to draw attention to myself, and an enormous ring was on my list of attention- getters—way, *way* down the list, probably right next to glitter nail polish, but still . . . attention-getter. So I told him to take it back. I didn't want it.

He didn't talk to me for two entire days. We only went back to being best friends after I repeated an apology he had written down on a napkin from the nacho bar at the 7-Eleven.

I, Justina Griffith, apologize for my rudeness in not accepting a gift from my awesome and oh-so-handsome friend Ian. Who might also possibly be magic. And therefore, hither and dither, former and latter, perfunctory and whatnot . . . I'll never do it again.

Ian is planning on becoming a lawyer one day. He likes to inject fancy nonsense words into his writing in preparation for his future career.

I thought the daisy ring topic was closed. Apparently not.

He stopped at a red light and turned to me. "I wanted to get a gift that meant something to you."

"The ring was enormous."

"You worry too much about everyone else."

"*Huge.* Like something out of a cartoon."

"Do what you want. Forget them."

"Like something a Muppet would wear."

"Justina."

"It was a Mutant Muppet ring."

He smirked.

So I kept at it. "ATeenageMutant...Muppet...Turtle . . . ring . . . for Ninjas." And there it was. The crease. Air.

"Justina." He said my name like he adored me but was also totally annoyed by me. There was something about that combination that made my heart melt through the pavement.

Ian reached over and massaged my neck. "Stop assuming the worst, would you?"

The neck massage: signature move of a Professional Boyfriend. Aaaaah.

But with these types of moves, he clearly could've landed any girl he wanted for a prom date. I couldn't explain why he had picked me, but since he had, he also deserved the truth.

I took a deep breath and blurted it all out at once. "Dan kissed me, he was trying to make Allyson jealous so he asked me to kiss him, I told him no, but he did it anyway, it felt like a car wreck, I didn't intend to kiss him, please don't—"

"I know."

"Please don't be mad."

"I'm not."

"Then how do you know that's what happened?"

"I know you. The last thing you would do is kiss Dan-O the Man-O to make someone jealous. That's something *he* would do. Not you."

I smiled. "Ian Clark! Did you just assume the worst of someone?"

"I didn't assume it. I *saw* it. There's a big difference."

I came close to telling him I tried to drag Allyson out of there by her ponytail. But I didn't want him to think I had psychotic jealous strands bubbling in my DNA.

He was being so forgiving of this crap with Dan. He was trusting. Calm. Sensible. But then again, maybe a *little* jealousy would've been nice. I mean, I kissed another guy and he didn't put up a fight? He didn't let Eva get away with it.

But of course, he'd been in love with her. Maybe he didn't feel a need to put up a fight for me. But then Ian pushed his hair away from his face, and that's when I could see his cheeks were flushed. "But maybe you could . . . you know . . . stay away from him?"

Touchdown! His jealousy DNA strands were alive and well! I don't know why this was reassuring, but it was. I scooched over as far as my seat belt would allow and grabbed his one free hand. "I'll dance to a Journey song with you tonight. *Our* Journey song."

His face opened instantly like a jack-in-the-box. "No protest?"

"I may even enjoy myself." Understatement. Our song was "Open Arms." It had become our song because I totally hated it. The cheese factor was huge— dumb lyrics, melodramatic, sweeping chorus. Which was why Ian loved blasting it on his car stereo and belting out the words while I covered my ears and hummed until the pain went away.

The day he asked me to prom, we had been sitting in his clunker Mercedes in the school parking lot. I was holding the letter he'd left in my locker:

Go to prom with me? Please? We could totally carpool.
Check the correct box: ___Yes

He had only given me one choice. And attached to the note was a daisy—a very persuasive technique. As far as Getting Asked To The Prom moments go, it was looking to be an A plus. But it was then that we'd had that conversation about going just as *friends*. Not my most favorite part of the memory. Fortunately, after that uncomfortable moment, he finally looked over at me and said, "You look pretty today."

Swoon.

Guys don't know the power we hold over them with the right tint of lip gloss. He didn't mention which part of me looked pretty, but I was pretty sure the Cherry Lip Smackers was to thank. So I puckered and sang the words from "Open Arms" to him, a cappella.

Maybe we were only going to prom as friends, but the smirk on his face while I sang told me we were going to have a great time.

Ian turned on his blinker and slowly steered the car into the parking lot of the Grand Riverside Hotel. "I'll make sure the DJ plays our song." He cut his eyes over to me. "We'll . . . we'll take things slowly. Okay?"

I could tell we were saying things we weren't quite ready to articulate. But we were getting there.

As the hotel came into view, my mouth dropped. "Wow" was the only descriptive word I could come up with. But I meant it. The hotel was massive and sparkled like a majestic mountain, lit with purple spotlights—the prom color Allyson had picked.

Ian didn't say anything. He just reached out and gently placed his hand on top of mine. It wasn't a hand *hold*, but it was close. Close enough. We were touching.

Butterflies.

We entered the grand ballroom and I gasped. Totally gasped, with my hand over my mouth and everything. The room was stunning—saturated and dripping with purple, black, and silver. We entered through silver archways and were amazed by the beautiful glowing lanterns, columns covered in silver sequins and lit from the inside, and a large population of purple balloons that seemed to be growing and multiplying by the second. Can balloons mate?

The room was gleaming. Brilliant. And totally romantic. Above the dance floor was an enormous purple paper lantern—I couldn't wait to stand under it and get my kiss from Ian—which was my newly concocted plan for The Moment of Lip Lock Bliss.

He placed his hand on my back—it was so natural, like we'd been a couple for years. "I told you this would be amazing."

I almost squealed, but took in quick, deep breaths to keep myself calm. *Be cool. Be cool.* "I may be warming up to this idea of prom." And as much as I didn't want to admit it, Allyson had done an amazing job.

"It's a lot better than supervising the front seat of my car, huh?" I shot him a wink. "There's some promise here."

"Dude, what the—" The Mikes had wandered up and were just as awed by the decorations. Mike surveyed the entire room. "Dude. It looks like a purple volcano erupted in here. The place is oozing . . . sparkly . . . molten . . . purple . . . lava. . . ."

Ian leaned over to him. "Dude."

The Mikes looked him over, then cracked smiles and answered with, "Duuuuuude."

I had no idea what any of this meant, but it was adorable.

We picked up our place cards to find out which table we were assigned to for dinner—table five. Since that was Ian's track uniform number, I assumed this was a good sign. A meant-to-be sort of thing. Then again, I could've been reaching, but I decided instead to stick with my "good sign" theory.

Before we sat down, Ian and I wandered around, checking out all the decorations and seeing who was there. I'll admit, I kept my eye out for Allyson and Eva—I did *not*

Hailey was across the room leaning on the wall next to the restroom, smacking her gum. A sure sign she was already over this scene.

"Go talk to her." Ian motioned to Hailey. "I'll get us something to drink."

He gently shoved me on my way, and I approached her hesitantly. She had a vacant stare again. "Still mad?"

She popped a bubble. "Not at *you*, anyway."

I leaned against the wall next to her, pleased with our vantage point—we could see everyone from this spot. "Did he admit to liking Allyson?"

"Yeah. On our way here in the car. The car *I* had to drive cuz the jerk did *eight* Jell-O shots! I knew he was drunk, but Lord!"

"Eight? Is he okay?"

"He's definitely not himself, that's for sure. And he's a crappy kisser."

"Wait. You *kissed* him?"

"He was all apologetic and sad, and he made a move so I let him." She gave a halfhearted shrug. "I had to. Otherwise I'd never know."

I nodded, totally getting what she meant.

"At least now I have my answer."

My eyes turned saucerlike. "And? Which category?"

"The worst. A combo."

"No."

Hailey winced. "Too much tongue *and* toothy."

"Sweet Jesus."

"Yeah, he moved in and crashed into my front teeth like it was the freaking derby. I felt like I needed to be wearing a seat belt."

I squirmed. "Oh, Hailey."

"Yeah, and then he flipped his tongue around in there like it was an eel. And not one of those cute ones you see on snorkeling trips."

"The worst."

"I know. But at least I can move on. Maybe with that hottie?" She motioned to the other side of the room.

Brian Sontag.

"Dark hair. By the DJ." She called him like a pool game— just like we always had. But I couldn't help but hope she was getting sick of the game, too.

"Brian? But he's with Allyson. Those two are pretty much our school mascot."

"I'm not dumb." She threw her shoulders back. "I think it's time to give Allyson Moore a taste of her own poison."

My instinct was for us to leave it alone. Ian and I were here together now—well, sort of, since he was actually over at the drink table at the moment. But Allyson was leeching on to Brian finally, so I had nothing to worry about.

Except that the words Allyson had said in Dan's kitchen flashed into my brain: *Oh, I have to talk to him.* And then how she had bombarded Ian by the pool with her long, boring stories, and how she had waved her arms all around for added drama. Was she trying to win Ian back?

I circled behind Hailey and gave her a nudge, like a mother horse. "Do it."

A wicked smile grew across her face. "Oh, yeah—it's on."

I pressed myself up against a wall, wishing for powers of invisibility while I watched Hailey work her magic. She sauntered right up to Brian and Allyson. Brian was nodding his head along to the music. Allyson was holding her compact mirror high in the air, trying to smooth a stray hair on her polished rock of a head.

It didn't take long. Only four words out of Hailey's mouth and she already had her hand on his arm. Dang, she was good.

Allyson snapped her compact shut and strutted off.

Yes! She was walking off in defeat! I suddenly felt like twirling a flag to commemorate the moment.

My eyes followed Allyson as she weaved in and out of people— her hips moving in a rhythmic motion, totally graceful—and made her way across the room to the back table. The *drink* table.

Wait. She wasn't walking away in defeat—she was using this moment to go find Ian!

My chest heaved and my heart jumped out of my chest, cannonball-style. Allyson tapped Ian's shoulder, and he turned around, a drink in each hand. Her back was to me, but I could tell Allyson was telling some boring story again, because her hands were flying.

Part of me wanted to rush over there and find out what Allyson was talking about. But I didn't have to.

Ian—eternal nice guy—just smiled, shrugged, nodded, then walked away. My muscles relaxed, and I could feel the sanity returning.

Hailey stepped up next to me. "I'm outta here."

"Why? What about Brian Sontag?"

"He doesn't talk much. Cute, but not much there."

I was proud of her. A year ago she would've kissed him and never questioned his brain capacity. He'd just be a tally. But now she was looking for something more. I draped my arm around her. "Smart move."

"Wanna ditch?" Her tone was hushed but very excitable. "We could go watch old *Buffy* episodes in our pajamas and eat licorice."

A *Buffy* marathon in pajamas was tempting. But Ian was approaching me with a cup of punch in his hand and an adorable smirk on his face. This night was shaping up to be one of the best of my life.

She assessed the situation, glancing at him, then me. "It's okay." She punched buttons on her phone. "I'm texting Mom to come get me."

"Hailey, no. You can't leave me!"

"This sucks. Mom will return my dress and I can use the money to buy *real* clothes. Cute clothes. Party clothes. For Lurch's tomorrow night. Wanna go together?"

More temptation. When Hailey asked me to go to parties, I'd salivate like Sol when there's a rib-eye steak nearby. Plus, Lurch's parties were the best. His parents were partial owners of the San Diego Chargers. Everyone knew the Chargers' schedule, and therefore, when his parents would be gone. Half the school would bombard his house in the country club—sometimes without Lurch even knowing it was going to happen. Usually he didn't even pay attention—he'd be downstairs in the basement on his computer playing World of Warcraft against some dude in Malaysia. Lurch was not the coolest cat in the village, but his parties rocked.

But then I remembered Ian asking me to go to Lurch's party with him. So we could Whatever that meant. I still didn't know.

"I'm supposed to go with Ian." I winced. "Maybe we could all go together?"

I felt a twinge. A shift. Discomfort. It was the rumblings of the dreaded third-wheel syndrome. That syndrome that creates the awkward moment when you realize your friendship is spiraling, changing, and you can either push through it together, or push each other away.

Then I saw it in her eyes. A sparkle. "Don't worry about it. I'll go solo," she said.

My face flushed with warmth. I knew we were going to have to deal with this at some point in our friendship . . . and it all happened right there in that tiny moment. She could have gotten upset. But she didn't.

Hailey shrugged off the conversation and casually looked around the room. Dan was on the dance floor. Doing the robot. "Aaaand prom is a horror movie," she said just before she popped a bubble.

Ian slowed as he neared us, and said, "I'll go put these on the table."

My eyes followed him as he walked away. "I hope you're wrong, Hailey."

He carefully set our drinks next to our forks, then moved them next to our knives. He liked to follow rules of etiquette, but he didn't realize anyone else noticed. Which was the definition of adorable.

"In your case," Hailey said, "I *am* wrong." She draped her arm over my shoulder. "I'm gone. Now kiss that boy tonight."

I hugged her, knowing she might be gone before the salads were served. "I'll call you later."

"Hopefully not!" She winked.

Ian was buttering his bread when I sat down next to him. The table was gorgeous, covered with a black tablecloth and a centerpiece that was a glass bowl full of purple beads, lit from below. No wonder the tickets cost ninety-five bucks.

I surveyed our table to see who we would be eating dinner with. There were eight seats at our table: Me, Ian, the Mikes, and their dates. Since I was their lab partner, I guessed sitting with the Mikes would make for easy school- related conversation. So far so good.

But two seats were empty: Hailey and Dan. I figured Dan was enjoying his buzz too much to sit down for bread and salad. He probably didn't even know he'd been ditched by Hailey.

Mike held up his cup of punch and toasted, "Thrilled to be in the company of such a stunning couple."

I blushed. A couple? Was he sensing something more between us? I only talked to the Mikes about chemistry, not the chemistry of my love life, so I couldn't help but be silent. And a little embarrassed.

Other Mike raised his cup too. "To you dudes." We clinked plastic cups while their gorgeous dates texted on their phones.

I couldn't blame them. It couldn't be fun hanging out in a ballroom full of Huntington High girls. I thought about saying hi to them, but I'd heard scary stories about Ledbetter girls—look at them wrong and they'll shred you to pieces.

I didn't know if they had heard the rude things Huntington girls said about them, but I knew they had already given me their best up-and-down unfriendly looks by Dan's pool. At least I *hoped* those were their best.

I kept my eyes on my fork.

Ian sliced a piece of bread for me. "You're gonna start getting cranky. You need to eat."

He was right. My stomach was growling. "Thanks for being Lord of My Blood Sugar." I picked up the bread to take a bite, but there wasn't any butter on it. I started to hand it back to him, but I noticed he was chewing his lip. Which meant something wasn't right. "What is it?"

"I talked to the DJ. He can't play our song. The school makes him play from a predetermined set list." Ian spread butter on my bread, lots of it, just the way I liked. "Our only option is a Justin Timberlake song."

"Eww." I made my pouty face.

"What?" He elbowed me. "You don't want to dance to 'SexyBack'?"

"If I have to." And to be honest, I really didn't mind at all.

I reached out to hand Ian another pat of butter for my bread, but something caught my eye. A cloud puff of pink.

Eva was headed right for us.

I imagined stuffing her pink dress into a shredder. Yeah, my imagination is ridiculous. I flattened my napkin out on my lap, then re-flattened it and pretended there was absolutely nothing unusual going on.

Nothing awkward. Nope, nope.

Eva knelt down behind Ian. "Can I talk to you?" She glanced over at me. "Oh, hi, Justina," she said with a brief dismissive nod.

Everyone knew Ian and I were just friends. I was no threat. It probably didn't even cross her mind that stealing him back right in front of my face would make me want to shred her pink puff of a dress.

But there would be no ridiculous dress shredding because Ian quickly turned around and faced her. "Eva," he said, as if she were a toddler, "I never want to talk to you again. Leave us alone."

Eva's eyes reddened. "But I—"

"Go. Away." He said it without emotion. He even went back to buttering my bread as if he had dusted away a gnat. No big deal. He was done with her.

"Here!" Eva tossed a folded note into his lap and stormed off, crying. She crumpled into the arms of Brianna Portman, who consoled her and dragged her across the floor, back over to Jimmy DeFranco's table, where they were all sitting together. Jimmy was chewing on bread, looking clueless. His faux- hawk had flopped over.

Ian opened the note carefully, like it might bite him. He read it, shook his head, and started to crumple it up.

I wanted to read that note so bad I would've put a mafia hit on someone just to get a glimpse. Ian must have seen my I-will-kill-someone-to-read-that face because he set it in front of me and said, "Read it. I don't mind."

So yeah, I read the thing, and if I had read it any faster I would've eaten it.

Ian, I am so sorry for hurting you. You deserve to be with someone better than me. One day you'll find that special girl.

*Peace & love, Eva *Luke 7:47-48*

"What's the Bible passage?" I asked.

He shrugged. "Forgiveness, I'm sure. They always are." He picked at some lint on his sleeve.

"Wow," I said, flattening the napkin on my lap again. "When you're done, you're done."

Ian took a deep satisfying breath. "Yep."

At that moment I actually felt sorry for Eva. Hearing Ian Clark say the words *I never want to talk to you again* would crush me. He was the one who listened to all of my babbling—he knew virtually everything about me. I could never let our friendship go.

My chest tightened. Oh my god. What were we doing? Kissing Dan wasn't my fault—but deep down, did I let it happen? Did I miss my partying kissing life too much? What if my need to kiss Ian ended up costing us our friendship? I'd never forgive myself. I would not allow myself to become the next Eva.

"Let's not do this," I said.

"Eat bread?" He flipped my piece over and began to double butter it. Forcefully.

"I can't handle you ever saying those words to me. What if you never wanted to talk to *me* someday?"

"She kissed another guy."

"So did I about an hour ago. Remember? And I know I'm not your girlfriend or anything, but I *am* your friend. And your date. What kind of person am I? You should run away while you still have the chance."

Huh. I went in the wrong direction with that. Telling him I'm not his girlfriend? Pretending like he should dump me? That was not how I wanted to steer this.

He pressed his lips together and dug deeper into the butter, shaking his head. He was frustrated. I knew all his looks—angry, sad, defeated. This was frustration. It was all in the eyebrows—tilty and uneven. As he lifted the knife, the butter took flight and landed with a thud.

Right under my armpit.

I barely even moved, just stared straight ahead. This was becoming routine for me. Ian quickly grabbed a cloth napkin and wiped it off, trying not to get too close to my boob, which was tucked into my extra-enhancing Miracle Bra. He could have easily copped a feel, and I wouldn't have stopped him, but he didn't. His being timid near my boob made me question whether he was *ever* going to explore there. The possibility seemed slim. Maybe *that's* why they called it a Miracle Bra?

"I'm not running away." Ian grabbed another fresh napkin and wiped one more time, getting off as much as he could. "Sorry, Justina." Then he went back to buttering my bread.

A smile filled my face. "I can do that. You don't need to be my personal bread butterer." It suddenly felt like we were one of those old couples who sat on rockers on the front porch, drank sweet tea, talked about the grandkids, and cut each other's meat.

He took a little nibble of my bread and raised a brow. "Too late."

Toe-dip.

My face flushed and my stomach orbited the rest of my organs—a feeling that gave me a slight buzz and a little seasickness. Whoa. Was this what they meant by lovesickness?

Wow.

If having Ian Clark for a boyfriend meant never kissing another guy, I'd sign that contract. I was in.

"I hate what Eva did to you." My stomach was still fluttering. "I'd never kiss another guy." Was this it? Was I putting it all out there? About to tell him how I really felt?

He turned away, looking embarrassed. "It's okay. You don't have to say this."

"I mean, I'd never *choose* to kiss another guy. I can't help it if some jerk drinks Jell-O shots and plants one on me. Even though I know I've gotten a reputation as an Excessive Kisser, but that's all in the past—"

"Shh."

"But it would never be my *choice* to kiss another—"

"Shh!"

"Ian! Don't shush me! I want to tell you this."

"I don't mean shush like stop talking. I mean shush like you don't have to explain." He leaned over and placed a perfectly double-buttered piece of bread on my plate. It glistened like it had been beamed down straight from heaven—an appetizer from the angels. "I trust you," he said. "Now eat."

Relief filled the air. Everything was so easy with him—it always had been. I was the one making it complicated.

Breathe in. Breathe out. Eat some freaking food. Your low blood sugar is making you crazy crackers.

I picked up the bread to take a bite, but I heard a strange squawking sound. Dan-O the Man-O was out on the dance floor all by himself, doing the chicken dance and some polka moves, and there wasn't even any music playing. The alcohol had clearly changed him—from a perfectly nice guy to a total boob.

"Let's party, people!" Dan stumbled across the floor toward our table, bopping his head and snapping his fingers like a character from an old *Saturday Night Live* skit. He mobbed Ian and me, hugging us from behind.

"Why don't you sit down, Dan?" Ian stood up to steady him. "You could use some food."

"Didja hear? Hailey ditched me. I'm solo, dude!"

Ian tried to guide him to his chair. "Sit down with us."

"No time to siddown. We gotta party, people. Let's go hottubbing. Time to get naked!"

"No. Not getting naked—sitting down." Ian tried to grab him by the arm to force him into the chair, but Dan twisted and squirted out of his grip.

Suddenly he was behind me, and I could feel his hand on my back. "Naw, dude! Naked!" And that's when I heard *zip!* And a gush of air rushed around my back. Dan had unzipped my dress.

UNZIPPED MY DRESS!

I immediately grabbed the sides and did my best to cover the important parts. Ian pushed Dan back. He lost it. He was done. "Get out of here!" He dragged Dan by the arm over to one of the chaperones. That was the end of Dan-O the Man-O's little one-man party.

But his drunken-zipper stunt had caused a serious dress malfunction. I reached behind me and discovered that the zipper was completely missing. He had pulled it right off!

Oh my god, oh my god. This can't be happening!

I rushed past Ian as he was handing Dan off to the vice principal, my zipper still dangling from Dan's hand. "Going to the bathroom!" I yelped. "Dress malfunction!!"

Ian yelled after me as I ran away. "Need help?"

"I need *girl* help!" The bathroom was empty, thankfully. It was the kind that had a front seating area, like a little living room. It was decorated with fancy Victorian love seats and thick maroon carpeting. There were endless drawers, huge mirrors, and perfect soft lighting. The room felt too fancy for me to be having such a redneck problem. No zipper? For real?!

I tucked the sides of my dress up under my armpits, squatted down low, and rifled through the drawers, trying to find anything to pin it back together. All I could find was a tampon. Not helpful.

I leaned against the wall, trying to hide my gaping back, when the door opened. And there were silver, strappy shoes. The Grecian goddess herself stood in front of me. I was having the worst dress malfunction of my life and Allyson Moore was going to witness it.

Dang it! She crossed her arms and looked down on me—literally. I had scrunched low in the corner, trying to look invisible, I guess.

"Ian sent me in here," she said.

Oh god, no. He sent freaking Allyson Flag Twirler Moore in here to help me fix my dress? Did he not care about my feelings at all? There were plenty of other girls out there he could have picked. But *her*? Did he think fixing a zipper could suddenly turn us into bosom buddies? Because that was never going to happen—our bosoms came from the opposite sides of the mammary track.

"I'm fine." I shook my head and turned away, looking into the corner. "I don't need anyone."

"Don't go all Tyra Banks on me. You need help."

I cut my eyes up at her. She stuck her hand on her hip. "You need a safety pin. A tampon is not going to work."

I glanced at my hand: oh lord, I was still holding it! Allyson reached into her straight-from-*Glamour*-magazine beaded purse and pulled out a safety pin. I'm sure her prom checklist included a section on survival items. Safety pin? Check. Evil scheme to steal someone else's boyfriend? Check!

"Thanks." I reached up and took it from her. "I got it from here."

"Really?" She shifted and put her hand on her other hip. She seemed to like punctuating her sentences with hip movements. "I'd like to see that." Another hip shift.

I tossed the tampon back in the drawer and tried reaching around to pin the top together, but nearly dislocated my shoulder.

"Relax. Turn around. This won't hurt." I slowly turned, realizing I was going to need her help. If Ian sent her in here, he must think she wants to be friends. But I needed to know for sure.

"Why did Ian send you?"

"He didn't, actually. I volunteered."

"But how did you know—"

"I could tell he was upset. You know, he had that pouty look." She pulled my dress together tight. "Hold still."

"*What* pouty look?" Why was Allyson acting like she knew the intricacies of Ian's looks? *I* was the one who knew all of Ian's looks!

"He had that look he always gets when he's concentrating," she said. "Like just before a track meet. He paces around getting all pouty. He wrinkles his eyebrows. It's cute."

"It's *not* cute."

"So you don't think he's cute?" She smirked. "Good to know."

"He's my date." I wiggled, and she pulled tighter. It was getting hard to breathe.

"You guys are just friends. What are you getting all upset about?"

"We . . . we're not just friends." Wow. That felt weird to say. I mean, it's not like I said we were boyfriend/girlfriend, but still. It was a public declaration of wanting to be . . . more.

Just then the safety pin holding my dress together popped. My dress fell to my waist. Allyson Moore got an eyeful of my boobs tucked in an extra-enhancing bra as they made their public appearance in the girls' bathroom mirror.

I yanked my dress back up and Allyson reached out. "Here, let me help—"

"No! I'll figure it out!"

"Fine." She dropped the broken safety pin back into her purse and zipped it closed. But not in your I'm-zipping-my-purse-like-a-normal-girl way. She zipped it slowly, so I could hear every click of the zipper.

She had a perfectly good zipper. I had none.

"Good luck tonight with Ian. I hope he thinks of you as more than friends, too." On the way out the door she turned back. "I'll go tell him your dress can't be fixed."

"Don't—"

But she was already gone. And off to have yet another talk with Ian. My date.

What did she mean she hoped he thinks of me as more than friends? Was she insinuating he didn't? No, no way. Ian wanted me to be his girlfriend.

I was almost sure of it.

Chapter Seven

FUNYUNS

I DON'T TELL Gilda and Donna the part where I considered tying my dress together with the tampon string before realizing the darn thing was too short. There are some parts they don't need to know.

"Tell me about this reputation of yours," Donna says.

That part, too.

Gilda eyeballs her. "Let's not go there."

Donna nonchalantly flips though a celebrity tabloid magazine. "I just think we have a bit of a mystery on our hands. Does Ian want to be her boyfriend or not? And in a juicy celebrity scandal, reputations are things that investigative reporters will, you know . . . investigate."

"They're not investigative reporters, Donna." Gilda gives her an irritated look. "They're tabloid jerks. And Justina's reputation has nothing to do with whether Ian loves her or not."

Loves me or not—it feels weird to think of him possibly being in love with me.

Or possibly not.

It also feels weird to have two grown women arguing over my love life. Because maybe there is no argument.

"Hold on." I put my hand up to stop their analysis. "Donna's right. My reputation does play a part in this. I don't know if it's been long enough for it to suddenly not be a part of me anymore."

Maybe that's why you did what you did, Ian? Lose me before I hurt you?

Donna stands next to me and puts her hand on my shoulder, like a TV game show host. "Let's do the math, doll."

I peer up at her. "Math? This early in the morning?"

She stuffs her hands in her pockets and walks back and forth the length of the counter. "Reputations can be erased by a simple mathematical formula. Take the number of infractions—so in your case, it's the number of excessive kissing incidents—and multiply it by 2.5."

Gilda shakes her head and laughs. "Why 2.5?"

Donna gives her a challenging look, radiating superiority, even though the two seem to be equally having fun with this. "Every time you do a misdeed you must do the right thing 2.5 more times because people don't just change their mind about you when you do the right thing twice. It has to be more than just a fluke. And multiplying by three is just a pain. So 2.5." They both stare at me as if they're waiting for an answer.

"What? Now? You want me to multiply the number of guys I've kissed by 2.5?"

They both nod energetically.

I mumble under my breath, "Fifty-two weeks in a year . . . multiplied by two . . . freshman year . . . add Jimmy DeFranco's pool party . . . multiply by 2.5 . . . carry the one . . ."

Gilda taps at her watch. "You already told me how many guys you kissed. Why is this taking so long?"

I bite at my lip. "I left out a few."

Donna puts her hand on my shoulder again, back to playing game show host. "And the total number of days until your reputation is erased?"

I quickly carry the one and add. "Two hundred and twenty days."

"Wow," Gilda says. "According to Donna's brilliant equation, Ian erased your reputation from his mind"—she looks up at the ceiling for a moment, then—"three weeks ago!"

I quickly add up the days to figure out when that would've been. "Oh my god." I can feel the blood rush out of my face and down to my feet. "Three weeks ago . . . that was the day Ian told me I looked pretty. I thought it was just the lip gloss. . . ."

Donna snatches a bag of Funyuns, rips them open, and gives me a satisfied wink. "Told ya."

We all happily munch on Funyuns because even the name implies things are looking up.

"As long as you didn't kiss another guy at prom or anything," Gilda adds. And the two of them laugh.

But I don't laugh with them. "Um. Does dancing with someone else count?" My voice is strained.

Gilda drops a Funyun and flops her head on the counter. "Aw, honey."

"It was an accident!" I say, hoping it isn't a lie.

Donna raises an eyebrow and inspects my face. "How does one *accidentally* dance with a guy?" It's clear to her I don't have an answer, so she steps back and says, "Wait, are you sure *you're* the one who got ditched?"

I readjust my skirt, making the stains and rips very visible. "Believe me, Ian ditched *me*," I say.

"So this dancing"—Gilda lifts her face to look over my dress—"is that how you ended up with that rip?"

I snatch one more Funyun and pop it in my mouth. "Nope, that happened over on Lexington Avenue. After the bruise and the tattoo and the thing that happened with the Chihuahua."

They both look at me like grandparents holding an iPhone . . . totally confused.

"Okay, so I accidentally danced with a guy just before I got this."

I point to a light brown stain. Thigh high.

Chapter Eight
RUBBERY CHICKEN MARSALA

AT THAT POINT, crying seemed like a ridiculous waste of time, given everything that needed to be done to get my dress back together. But it was the only solution I could come up with.

Just then two girls came into the bathroom. Platform heels. Animal print dresses. Mike's and Other Mike's girlfriends—the Ledbetter girls.

I was scrunched in the corner trying to stifle my tears, but they didn't notice me. They were already mid-conversation.

"So? His *thing*. Is it, you know . . . *big*?"

"Like a zucchini!"

"Really? Which kind?"

"What do you mean which kind? The stir-fry kind."

I stayed small and quiet, not wanting to interrupt their conversation. The brunette fluffed up her hair in the mirror. "No, I mean like is it the mutant ginormous overripe kind you see at the state fair? Or is it one of those wimpy Italian zucchinis?"

I did not want to know the answer to that question. Mike was my lab partner, for chemistry's sake! "Hi," I interrupted. My voice must have sounded like a talking mouse in the corner.

They both turned to each other. "Did you hear something?"

"Yeah. Eerie. Is this place haunted?"

"Down here," I said, and they both looked down at me, probably relieved I wasn't a small ghost.

The blond one said, "Didn't you come in here to fix your dress? Like a *while* ago?" Her tone was sharp. "Why are you just sitting on the floor?"

"The girl Ian sent in here was—"

"And dinner is almost over," the brown-haired one chimed in. "Ian wasn't too happy about eating alone."

Oh no. Why didn't I just let Allyson help me? I could've been done, safely pinned into my dress and much closer to Ian's lips if I'd just let her help. I needed to stop worrying about what Allyson thought about Ian. Except she seemed to have *lots* of thoughts about Ian. I made an attempt to explain all this to the Ledbetter girls. "But the girl who tried to help me, she . . . she—"

"She what?" The blond girl squinted her eyes. "She smooshed you into a corner?"

"No, she was telling me about Ian's different facial expressions, like she knew him, you know, *really* knew him, and I assumed that she...you know..."

Their faces were pinched. Like I wasn't making any sense.

Crap. Me and my assumption problem. It always got in the way. I couldn't believe I'd left him alone for most of dinner because of my assumption addiction. The first step was admitting it. So there. I admitted it.

But I needed to get back to Ian and admit it to him— which meant I was going to have to get help from the Ledbetter girls. Even though I was a little worried they actually *were* going to smoosh me into the corner. Rumors about Ledbetter girls led me to think they were the smooshing type.

So I decided to go with the gracious approach. "I could really use some help. If you happened to have a safety pin in your purse, that'd be fantastic, um . . . I'm sorry, I don't know your names."

The dark-haired one cocked her head. "I'm Skank. And this is my friend Ho."

And with that, the rift between Ledbetter and Huntington girls was on the table, open for discussion. I held my dress up as I wobbled and stood to face them.

"Listen, I don't know why the girls at my school say bad things about Ledbetter girls, but—" I was trying to make my point about not being like the other Huntington High girls by adding some dramatic hand gestures but that's when my dress fell down yet again. "Oh, sweet God, when will you give me a break?" I whispered straight up at the ceiling.

They studied me carefully as I wriggled like a caterpillar, trying to get my stained, zipperless dress to stay up. I think it suddenly dawned on them there was no explanation needed. . . . I was not a typical Huntington girl. It didn't take an expert to see this dress did not include a designer label.

The dark-haired one dug around in her purse that looked more like an overnight bag. "I have an idea." She rooted for a long time and eventually got sidetracked. "Oh my god, look at this picture of me and Mike up at the lake."

Her friend nodded. "Hot. Does he shave his chest?"

Wow, they were into details. I cleared my throat. "Find anything to fix my dress?"

"Yeah, see, here's the thing." She put her purse/overnight luggage on the counter and looked down at me—I was back to scrunching low against the wall. "Mike is always using this particular type of wire to scrape wax off his board—says it's better than those plastic scrapers. The boy is obsessed with homemade surf accessories. Even made his own outdoor shower with laser lights installed."

"That shower is a party all itself," her friend added.

I fake coughed. "My dress?"

"Your dress. Right, so that wire would be the perfect thing to sew your dress back together." She snatched her purse back and rooted some more. "Here it is!" She pulled out some wire and bent off a piece about a foot long. "Let's get on our Martha skills!"

They spun me around, and the dark-haired girl said, "I'm assuming you don't mind if we ruin your dress?"

I shook my head. "Not at all. It may even look better."

They both worked on punching through the fabric with the wire and lacing it together so that it stayed up. They hummed and giggled while they worked—like members of Snow White's clan.

"Thanks, you guys," I said. "I don't even know your names. I mean, your *real* names."

"Serenity."

"Bliss."

I don't know what I was expecting, but not that. "Were you . . . were you both *born* with those names?"

"Nah, Mike and Mike call us by our *essence*. Not our names."

As freaky as it sounded, it was also rather sweet.

"That's why we came to your prom tonight, not ours," Serenity said. "Any guys who call us by our essence are guys we want to follow." The girls nodded and winked at each other.

"You mean it's Ledbetter prom tonight, too?"

Serenity yanked on my dress to squeeze it tight. "Yep. But I had to come to this one. Mike was so excited about your prom color. Purple. His favorite shade of lava lamp."

"What's the Ledbetter prom color?"

"Skin." Serenity spun me around. "Done! Check you out, lady."

I could see the back of the dress in the mirror—it actually looked cool. A little punk now. I liked it. "Thanks. I think Mike and Other Mike are right about your essences."

"Thanks, Sweetness." Serenity turned back to Bliss. "Now let's go dance!"

They both threw their hands in the air and howled. I half howled with them. No—more like a wimpy screech.

As we walked out, the girls were adorable and giggly, and I was still stained, sober, and sewn together with wire. To make matters worse, the dinner tables had been cleared and the dance floor was jammed with people. I had completely missed dinner! Even worse, Ian was nowhere to be seen.

Oh, no. No, no, no. Why didn't I let Allyson help me? I had to find him.

But Serenity and Bliss grabbed me by either arm and dragged me out to the dance floor. They joined up with Mike and Other Mike and kissed for an uncomfortably long time. They had already lost interest in me, so I stepped away from their smooch fest and stood at the edge of the floor, looking for Ian.

I scanned the crowd and finally saw him. He was at the far side of the room by the exit sign, facing the other direction talking on his cell. "Ian!" I called out, waving my purse in the air. But he couldn't hear me over the music.

"Wanna dance?"

It was Brian Sontag—stocky, with a fresh buzz cut, and gleaming white teeth. He glanced over to the other far side of the room, where Allyson was standing. On *her* cell phone.

"Our dates are busy." He gave me an energetic grin. "No reason why we can't have one dance."

Was he hitting on me?

Brian started swaying, and I couldn't think of a single word to say. All I could do was ping my head back and forth from one side of the room to the other, trying to figure out if Ian was talking to Allyson. What was going on?

But then again, I was the one on the dance floor in close vicinity to a swaying Brian Sontag. The last thing I needed was for Ian to think I was dancing with another guy. But I needed to know if he was talking to her. Surely it was a coincidence. "I gotta talk to Ian." Brian tried to respond, but I was already hauling it to the other side of the room. I pushed past people, weaving in and out like a basketball point guard, trying to get to Ian quickly. I reached the exit sign where he was standing, but it was an empty space. He was gone.

I dashed around the ballroom looking for him, calling his name out like he was a missing puppy. "Ian? Ian?!" But nothing. Out of desperation I hunted down Eva, worried that maybe he was with her. But I spotted her in a corner holding up a mirror for Jimmy while he smoothed the stray strands on his floppy faux-hawk.

Allyson was now on the dance floor with Brian. They were dancing, but not too close—no body parts touching. Maybe she *wasn't* talking to Ian? Maybe I had come down with a severe case of date-stealing paranoia?

Then it hit me: Ian must have gone out to the car to get my peanut butter cookie. Since I'd missed dinner, he'd know I'd be starving, and he took his role as Lord of My Blood Sugar seriously.

My stomach growled and led me away to find leftovers somewhere, because when my brain isn't thinking straight, my stomach takes over as Head Commander.

That's when I heard the clink of dishes. The waitstaff was cleaning up the dinner and taking plates off to the kitchen, whooshing quickly in and out of the swinging kitchen doors. I made my way across the room and stood near a waiter carrying a large tray of empty plates. Except there was one plate still full. The entire meal was untouched. It was mine. My stomach was in full commando mode, and it was taking too long for Ian to bring me a cookie.

"Excuse me?" I stepped closer and leaned in to get the waiter's attention. "I know this sounds weird, but I was stuck in the bathroom during the entire dinner and I didn't get to eat mine. Could I just have a taste?"

"Of course." He laid the tray down and handed me my dinner. But another waiter swung through the kitchen door at that exact moment and smacked right into him.

The plate flew, food hurtled through the air, and yet another stain came to town and made its new residence on my dress. Chicken Marsala. Thigh-high.

I rushed to the bathroom—*again!*—and tried my best to scrub it off. It was the same drill: search around the overly decorated bathroom/living room for something to fix my ridiculous problem.

There were no paper towels, only air dryers with stickers that said, "This is an environmentally friendly bathroom." The environment is super great and all, but couldn't Al Gore have agreed to provide some freaking paper towels for all the pathetic stain-covered girls on prom night?

Everyone who passed through had an opinion. One girl suggested using ice water, and another said soda water, and another said apple cider. It didn't matter—it was pointless. I had to face reality: my dress attracted flying liquid. And I'd managed to spend virtually my entire prom night in the bathroom, and not attached to Ian's lips. This was a disaster.

After eyeing the tampons again, I gave up on ever getting my dress looking presentable, and shuffled back out to the ballroom. I scanned the crowd, looking for Ian, but no luck. Cookie retrieval did *not* take that long. Where was he?

I reached for my phone to call him, but the crowd started getting wild and my ears filled with thunderous music. Everyone was juking around, jumping up and down to some old-school heavy metal, and based on Mike and Other Mike's excitement, I guessed they were stoked the song was on the school-sanctioned playlist. Even the school counselor was bopping her head to the beat.

Without realizing it, I suddenly started to sway. Maybe a little twirl, too. I couldn't "Hey, it's my new dancing partner." Brian Sontag was suddenly next to me, bouncing his head to the music.

Was he *everywhere*?

The counselor scooted next to us. "You guys make a cute couple."

Oh my god, she thought we were dancing together.

Wait. He was swaying. I was twirling next to him . . . we *were* dancing together! Had anyone else seen?

Hearing the word "couple" jolted me back to reality, and I stopped swaying. "It's nice of you to ask. But your girlfriend probably wants to dance with you."

"Not really," he said with a tinge of bitterness. He gave me a half smile as I started to walk away.

"Sweetness!" Other Mike spotted me and yanked me back onto the dance floor. "Get out here now and enjoy these tunes." He was yelling over the crowd. "Where's Ian?"

"I don't know!" I yelled into his ear.

"Ohhhhh." He gave me a thumbs-up, faking that he heard what I actually said.

So I shrugged, realizing we weren't going to get any further with this conversation, but when I turned to leave I ran smack into a polished rock—Allyson Moore's head.

"He's gone."

The music was so loud I could hardly hear her, but it almost sounded like she'd said he was gone. "What?" I leaned in, cupping my ear.

Just then the music softened—a slow song. A soft song. *Our* song. "Open Arms."

How was this possible? Did Ian get the DJ to play it? Bouncing on my toes, I popped up like a marmot, trying to find him.

"Ian left!" she yelled.

My feet dropped flat on the ground and stuck—hard— like an Olympic gymnast.

Thunk.

"What do you mean he left? Where'd he go?" I could feel my Creepy Cat Lady face coming on, all twitchy with my eyeballs darting around the room.

"He couldn't find you. He went to do a favor." She motioned her hand at Brian to come join her, as if this conversation was now boring her. "Ian seems to have lots of friends. Nice of him to do favors on prom night."

Brian followed directions and joined Allyson. She put her arms around his neck, and they showed actual physical contact, affection almost, as they swayed to our song.

Wait. Ian. *Left me?* I knew I took a long time in the bathroom, but . . . what?

He left to go do a *favor?* Who would ask him to do a favor on *prom night?*!

I swallowed hard. Crap. A nausea tsunami came over me, and I spun around to get away, but Other Mike grabbed my arm and stopped me. "Ian needs to get in here. I did that favor for him," hesaid.

"What favor?" Jesus, what was up with all the favors?!

"The DJ. He's a customer of mine. He's playing your song right now." As if I didn't know?

"I know!" I yelled. The twitch and my darty eyes were back.

No. No, no, no, no. This couldn't be happening. This moment was planned, severely thought out, mapped on my GPS if he would've let me...and he was just...*gone?* This was when I was going to get my answer. His kiss—proof he was total boyfriend material.

Everyone was paired up and slow dancing to our song while I stood in the middle of the room alone. I clutched my purse and held it to my chest like a shield—wishing Ian and I were the ones the chaperones had to separate. The thought of missing The Moment of Lip Lock Bliss with Ian was unbearable. It would've been an amazing kiss.

My heart started beating erratically. It flipped and took a nosedive. I pressed on my chest to remind it to keep pumping. It hurt—ached—as I silently wished for Ian to show up, make the dashing rescue and bring this sad moment to a romantic conclusion.

But no. Ian was not running in to scoop me into his arms. He was out doing favors. Hailey was right. Prom is a horror story. I bolted from the dance floor and dashed out the lobby doors to the parking lot, then stood on my toes looking for Ian's car. I analyzed every headlight and every engine sound, trying to figure out if he was there. But no. His rumbling old piece-o-crap Mercedes was nowhere to be found.

My phone vibrated. I rummaged through my purse and finally found it. I had a text message. From Ian.

Be back soon. Did A tell you? Taking longer than thought.

He didn't define "soon." He didn't tell me where he was. And he referred to Allyson as "A" as if they were close. A thing. French lovers. Soul mates from another lifetime.

The jerk! How could he do this?!

I quickly dialed Hailey. But she didn't pick up. I left a loud to-the-point message.

"I want a *Buffy* marathon!!!"

I took a deep breath and forced my integrity back to the surface for a moment. And I texted him back. *Where are you?* I waited and watched as people strolled in and out of the hotel, probably visiting their cars for a quick drink or a cigarette. I waited some more. I checked my phone. I checked it again. And again. No text back.

No text.

No text.

I stepped off the curb and hurried over to the side so I wouldn't be seen with tears pouring down my face. There I was, crying by myself in the parking lot on prom night. . . . Pretty much the definition of the World's Most Pathetic Moment.

It was all because of my expectations. Ridiculous expectations. I had actually thought Ian was a Professional Boyfriend. Why didn't it ever occur to me that maybe he just wanted to be friends with me? Not *be* with me.

But none of this made sense. What was going on? He was flirting with Allyson Moore? He left me here alone? He was a jerk?

But part of me still believed in him. I *knew* Ian. He was the type to swoop in and save the day. So where was the swooping?

"Wanna cigarette?"

A limousine driver was leaning against a long black Escalade, holding out a pack of Marlboro Lights. I didn't even realize I'd been crying and making crazy talk right there next to the limo.

"I don't smoke," I muttered.

"Thought it might calm the nerves. You seem a little . . . distracted." He leaned back on the hood.

"Um, I think someone's in there." I pointed to the back window, which was now fogging up.

"Yep. They seem to be having fun." Then he leaned forward like he was sharing a secret. "That girl's dad gave me two bills to make sure she had a good time."

Some giggling seeped out of the back window.

"Looks like you did your job," I said to this weirdo limousine driver.

He took a long drag on his cigarette. Then: "Yep, I love my job. I see a lot of crazy stuff."

"I bet," I said, glancing around, trying to think of a way out of this conversation.

But he didn't seem to want to stop talking.

"Yeah, sometimes I'm a driver, but most of the time I'm a therapist."

I perked up at that. "You mean couples spill their problems to you? And you give them advice?"

"Sure. I've helped plenty of couples in that limousine. I oughta charge a bundle."

Advice—from an outside party. That's what I needed. Not from a friend. Not from Mom. Not from pet psychology. Not from prom magazine editors. I needed someone who'd tell me like it is. "Could I ask you a question?"

"Fire away."

"How do you know if a guy is serious? Like if he wants you to be his girlfriend?"

"Go through the checklist."

"Checklist?"

He stomped his cigarette out on the pavement. "One. Do you have an active sexual relationship?"

"What? No!"

"Okay, okay, I just needed to establish a baseline. I wasn't sure how far things had gotten already. I'm guessing not far."

"Not far at all! That's why I'm asking you if you think he's interested in more. I would think an active sexual life would mean an automatic yes."

"Not necessarily," he said under his breath. "Let's start a little easier. Has he ever said you're pretty?"

"Yes," I said, as I thought about that perfect tint of lip gloss he'd noticed, and already feeling good about this checklist.

"Okay, but has he ever picked out something special about you? Like commented on your eyes?"

I paused, trying to remember. Nothing. I shook my head.

"Lips? Waist?"

"Waist?"

"As a reason to touch you, some guys will do that. You know, 'Gosh your waist is so oval,' then *boom*, hands on." It sounded a little creepy, but also quite nice. But of course, I had only experienced lower back touching, not waist touching.

"No." And all I could think about was that late-night phone conversation after the Sadie Hawkins dance. Ian mentioned Allyson's lips. He could pick out something special about her. But not me?

"Huh." The driver looked up at the sky like he was trying to pluck something from the stars. "Oh! Has he ever bought you a gift, like a super nice piece of lingerie? Or jewelry?"

No to the lingerie—we aren't forty. But there was jewelry—the daisy ring, of course. Except it was one of those vending machine type rings you get at the exit of a Shoney's. Not like a piece of jewelry all the other Huntington High girls were accustomed to—the kind that cost as much as my annual clothing allowance.

The limo driver must have deduced my answer to that question, because I was looking at my empty ring finger, not at him, so he asked one more question.

"Almost done." He crossed his arms. "Has he ever said anything like 'Let's take it slow' or 'I want to move slowly' or used the word 'slow' in any fashion with your name in the same sentence?"

The conversation in my driveway. When I said I wanted us to dance together, and he said "let's take things slowly," I had assumed he didn't want to rush me. I winced. "That isn't a good thing?"

He slid out a new cigarette, took a deep breath, and shook his head. "Sounds like you got your answer."

"But I could've sworn he wanted to get serious. This doesn't make sense!"

"Are we talking about the same guy who asked you to prom?"

"Yeah. Ian."

He glanced around the parking lot, pretending to look for him. "Ian, the guy who isn't here anymore?"

I flopped my head and thrust my empty hand at him. "I'll take that cigarette now." Not that I'd smoke it, but whatever.

But before he could hand it over, the back door of the limo flew open. Two people spilled out, laughing and falling on top of each other. Brianna Portman and Jimmy DeFranco.

Oh gross, no.

Brianna's smile became a scowl when she saw me standing there. I turned and headed back into the hotel. But she caught up with me. "Our secret. Got it? Or I'll tell Ian all about your little kiss with Dan by his hot tub. We all saw it."

I shrugged but didn't say a word.

"It's not like people won't believe me."

I squinted my eyes, making it clear her words didn't matter to me, even though they did.

"Reputations, Justina. You can't just lose them. They *stick*." She turned and looped arms with Jimmy, then added, "Don't run from it. Embrace it." Her scowl turned to a smirk, and not the cute, supportive kind . . . the ugly, fake kind.

She had clearly embraced her own reputation. And she seemed to enjoy the fact that I had one too. Like it made her feel more human to not be the only one.

I so badly wanted to say, "I'm done. I'm not the girl with the reputation anymore!" But I didn't. Instead I spoke softly, defeated. "Forget it. Our secret."

She winked at me and leaned over to whisper, "The limo driver's kinda cute. Go for it."

Brianna and Jimmy pushed through the main doors—he smacked her on the butt, she blew him a kiss, and they walked away in opposite directions.

I hovered near a bush by the entrance, trying to decide whether to go back in. I picked up my phone, pressed Ian's number, then hung up. I did that three more times before dropping the phone back in my purse. What was I supposed to say? "Get back to this party so you can continue being just friends with me"? So we can "take things slow" and I can get back to being boyfriend-less with a reputation? So you can stare at Allyson's lips?

No, I wasn't going to beg him to like me. And I was not going to chase him.

Prom must have been coming close to an end because herds of people began to fill the parking lot.

"Let's get outta here!" Brian yelled as he ran out the front door, holding hands with Allyson. They both slowed down when they saw me. The spotlight shining on the building reflected off a window and caught the sparkle in their crowns. Like they were perfect wedding cake toppers.

"See you at the after-party?" Allyson asked.

"Don't think so."

"You need a ride?" Brian asked. "Got plenty of room."

"No." I gripped my purse tightly. "Ian will be back soon."

Allyson tilted her head as if she were about to say something. Her mouth popped open for a brief moment, but she clamped it shut and gave me a dinky hand wave as she trotted off. The two of them hurried through the parking lot, and he held the door open for her. But her hands were flailing while she babbled on about something unimportant—probably about how unimpressed she was that they were in a *car* not a limo, I'm sure. He looked up at the sky a lot.

I didn't know a Prius could squeal, but Brian managed to skid his little punky tires and haul it out of that parking lot. Everyone else rushed through the doors, all headed somewhere. Certainly not home. And it hit me that I had just completely missed the prom. The whole thing. No food, no slow-dances, no kisses. Just two more stains and one less date. How did this happen?!

"Need a ride, sweet lady?" It was Serenity. The two Mikes and their dates had walked up, looped arm in arm. They were smiling and giggling.

"Wait." Serenity held her hand up. "Where is Ian? We can't leave without him."

I held out my phone, showing her our text messages. "Still haven't heard back from him." I flopped my head down, my eyes watered, and everything went blurry. "I think I got ditched."

"Aww, girl." Serenity put her hand on my shoulder. "We're going to In-N-Out. You should come with us!" Her voice was upbeat and persuasive—like she'd make a good car commercial announcer.

Other Mike was giggling, but he managed to get the words out. "Will you drive us, Sweetness?"

I kind of wanted to stomp on his foot and tell him to stop calling me that—I wasn't some "suh-weet" party girl. Not like before.

But then again, *Sweetness* sounded kind of nice. Unlike anything else that had happened tonight.

I shrugged. "I don't have a car." My voice was high- pitched and giddy—I sounded like I'd totally lost my mind. "My jerk of a date left me."

"You know how to drive a Cadillac." Mike quickly handed over his keys. "Everyone does, right?"

How disappointing. I couldn't believe The Mikes were luxury car owners, too. Couldn't they have at least owned a van? Something with a teardrop window and frosted glass? Something *interesting*?

I glanced out into the parking lot. All the cars were driving away, and not one single car was driving in. Ian wasn't coming back for me.

"Do you want us to take you home?" Bliss patted my face with a tissue, then patted her own face, I'm not even sure why. But it felt nice.

I stood up tall and took a deep breath. This night was not going to be ruined by Ian. He wasn't going to ditch me and force me to go home with my tail between my legs. That was for Sol. And even though I missed my adorable person of a dog, I wasn't ready to go home. Plus, I was starved, and Mom's leftover fundraiser curry didn't sound appetizing.

"We're going to In-N-Out," I announced as I jingled the keys to the Cadillac. "I'm driving."

Chapter Nine
NUTTY BAR

"YOUR SONG IS 'Open Arms'?" Donna has a wide grin.

"Yeah, it's cheesy, I know, but—"

"I love that song. You got good taste, doll."

Gilda edges closer to me, leaning in. "So he ditched you to do a favor?"

I nod. "I didn't know what kind of favor, but I knew I wanted to unhinge the mother of all lectures on him."

"Would you?"

"Would I lecture him? I'm not his mother or anything, but I mean..."

Oh, gosh. Was I needing to be hyper-involved? Get in the middle of *every* decision he made?

Gilda looks at her fingernails and says all casually, "Maybe we should talk about your parents. What's their relationship like?"

Oh, come on. This has to be the standard textbook question she asks all of her convenience store patients. She really thinks my parents' relationship has some huge bearing on my day-to-day behavior?

"They're fine. All good," I say. "This is . . . look, they have nothing to do with—"

Both Donna and Gilda fold their arms. They aren't letting me squirm out of this one.

And so I tell them. I tell them that my parents' paths hardly ever cross—she's so busy with her philanthropies, and he's always training dogs of people who know famous people. When they're apart, I get all of Mom's attention—too much of it, actually, but then when he calls, her world halts and she organizes him in a way that keeps him from getting lost in the world: flight schedules, bank account balances, oil changes. And when they are finally together in a room, they talk incessantly about all the minutiae—every moment and feeling and thought they've had while they were apart, and all of this is usually done between hugs and long kisses—the kisses seem to be Mom's favorite because she goes for those whenever she's not talking or breathing. But it's as if I don't exist. I sit in the corner with my hand raised, and part of me is grossed out by all of this and part of me is relieved to know my parents are still hot for each other. "Weird. Confusing. Whatever. There it is," I say, and breathe in deeply.

Gilda smiles. "I understand now."

"You do? Then please, tell me."

"In charge of the details? Talks about every thought and feeling? Loves kissing?" She twirls her braid around her finger, clearly enjoying this. "Sounds like someone in this very room."

Oh crap. I thought I'd be, like, thirty before I turned into my mother. I'm too young for this.

"Here's the thing." Donna gives me a focused stare. "Men want to be mothered. Nobody will tell you that truth, but Donna Kramer will. Men want Sexy Kitten in the wee hours of the night, and then again in the early hours of the morning—as inconvenient as that may be—but pretty much during the rest of the day, they want to be told what to do because *they don't know what to do*! They don't even know how to sort the lights from the darks!"

I consider telling her about Ian's intricate system for separating clothes—whites, extreme whites, warms, warm & cozies, darks, and sweaty uniforms. I consider telling her that Ian is the one who always seems to take care of me. I consider telling her she's wrong about him.

Even though, in a way, I wish she were right.

Why don't you fit the mold, Ian? If only you really were Captain Scumbag, like the rest of them. This would be black or white—it would be so simple.

"For example," Donna continues, "Rudy Jenkins, biggest slob this side of the Ledbetter Community Center. He'd drop his pants before even closing the front door and expect me to pick them up, and I'd be all 'O.M.God, hire a maid, Rudy!'"

"That's O.M.G." I try to correct her.

"Exactly! He wanted a mother! You get what I'm saying, right?"

I do. But I don't want to. "Yes."

Gilda tries to change the subject. "So you went to In-N- Out with your new friends?"

I nod. "In the Cadillac."

"A Caddy, eh?" Donna says with a wink. "Classy."

"I'm getting a good feeling about this." Gilda steps back and folds her arms contentedly, like she's solving a mystery. "My guess is these were nice people and they helped you find Ian at the restaurant."

"Have you been following along, Gilda?" Donna throws her arms in the air. "Our doll here drove off with a bunch of drug push-ers and she clearly didn't find Ian because why else would she be here telling this fascinating story to us while eating a Nutty Bar." She snatches a yellow box from below the counter. "Want a Nutty Bar? My treat."

Gilda rings up the Nutty Bar and puts her own money into the cash register, then passes the box on to me.

"Thanks." I grab the box and rip it open. "But you're both wrong . . . and you're both right."

Donna widens her stance and folds her arms.

"My friends aren't drug pushers. They're nice. And I did hear from Ian at In-N-Out."

"You did?" Gilda looks surprised.

"He called. But he didn't call *me*." I readjust myself on the stool. "And that's when I got this—" I lift up my skirt to show the bruise.

Donna squints as she bends over to get a better look. "Someone bruised you with a french fry?"

"That's what I thought at first, too." I shake my head, not wanting to recall this memory. "But no, this bruise was definitely not caused by a french fry."

Chapter Ten

SIZE SEVEN SILVER, STRAPPY JIMMY CHOO HEELS

THE CADILLAC.

After a closer look, I realized this was no regular Huntington High luxury automobile. And actually, I decided I would have preferred a van. Even a creepy, windowless, serial-killer van would've been more approachable than this dilapidated deathmobile.

Mike had borrowed it from his brother. And by "it" I mean a hooptie baby blue Caddy with a rusted-out hood and two windows missing. I had to admit . . . it was *interesting*.

"My bro is gonna demolish this thing in derby next week." Mike patted the roof like it was family. "We get one last night on the town with this gorgeous babe."

Serenity and Bliss squealed. They were very excitable. I yearned for their energy.

Other than the front seats, the Cadillac was practically a hollowed-out shell, full of metal and wires and empty bottles. "There's no backseat," I pointed out.

"Can't have seats in there for derby. But check it out— *coolers*." Mike busted open the back door (it required busting since mere opening would have gotten him nowhere), and he demonstrated how two large coolers could be pushed together to be used for beverage storage *and* comfortable seating.

Serenity, Bliss, and Other Mike climbed in and settled on top of the coolers, which didn't look all that comfortable.

Getting situated in the driver's seat took a little bit of gymnastics since there was a deep crack in the leather, from the seat all the way up to the headrest. I had to lean on the right side of my butt to avoid being manhandled by the seat leather.

"And also," Mike continued as he stuck the keys in the ignition, "don't let go of the steering wheel while you're driving. Otherwise Beast will make a U-turn on his own."

"'Beast'?"

He wrinkled his face. "You'll see."

I turned the key in the ignition. "This should be fun." But it wouldn't start.

Mike was now busy winking at Serenity. I tapped his knee. "It's not starting."

He snapped out of flirting mode and looked at me, spacing out for a bit like he was trying to remember something of critical importance. And then it came to him: "And also, you have to put a foot on the brake *and* the accelerator at the same time to get it to start." His face filled with relief, as if he'd just saved the world, and he went back to his favorite chore of winking at Serenity.

It was an awkward position, but putting a foot on both actually worked. We rambled down the road, and I gripped the steering wheel tightly, which really did want to go the other direction—Beast felt like he was coming alive.

And then I smelled the smoke, which started to pour out of the dashboard where the

"No, we don't light up in the car." "I mean the car . . . it's on *fire!*" For a moment he stared at the dashboard in a daze, then must have realized this was *actual* smoke and snapped out of it. "Crap!"

Was this how it was all going to go down? *Girl, sixteen, dies in fiery Beast inferno after being ditched at prom. Sources say she had been lip-deprived for over eight months. All the pathetic details at six.*

Luckily, that was not what happened, because in a totally sweet maneuver, Mike whipped out a small fire extinguisher from under the seat and doused the dashboard with foam. Some of it sprayed on my dress, but I didn't care. I was alive. And my kissless-prom death story would not headline the six o'clock news.

"Hmm." Mike scratched his ear. "My bro told me I might need this thing. Now I know why." Then he shot me a big smile and went back to finish his championship round of Serenity-winking. That girl seemed to be the proud owner of all of Mike's attention.

Must be nice.

As I drove down the road, I snuck glances in the rearview mirror of the three in the backseat—Serenity and Bliss were singing a song into the end of a lipstick tube and Other Mike was holding his arms out for balance as he teetered on the cooler.

But then my inner rule-follower kicked in, and I poked at Mike. "Wait, isn't it illegal for them to be sitting in the back like that? Without seat belts?"

He smiled a big toothy smile. "And also, if you see a cop, yell *duck*."

I had to yell duck twice. Mike was not the best front- seat-cop-heads-upper. He was highly distractible. But at least my backseat passengers were good listeners and they ducked when they were told.

We were not the only ones with the brilliant idea to get food at the In-N-Out. Apparently, no one had eaten the chicken Marsala, and the line backed up to the door.

Mike shook his head. "Bummer, dudes."

The place was packed with Huntington High prom runaways, their clothes looking a little rumpled now: ties undone, shirts untucked, shoes missing. But still, no one seemed to look as filthy as I did. And certainly no one was sporting a dress sewn together with wire. Oh embarrassment, how you taunt me.

Other Mike leaned up and gripped Mike's shoulder. "We're waiting, dude."

"It'll take too long. There are plenty of options, bro. I hear the Big Boy is open till midnight."

"Dude. It's In-N-Out. Toasted buns. Natural cut fries. I'm not going *anywhere*."

"Bro . . ."

"Dude."

Mike sighed.

"Fine."

It was amazing what those two could quickly resolve with their bro/dude conversations. How much time this world wastes with excessive syllables.

We joined the throngs of wilty prom people, and as we waited, I stepped out of line to get a glimpse of the menu sign. My mouth was watering at the picture of the Double- Double cheeseburger— the cheese part, not the burger part. But then I lost my appetite when I noticed Allyson and Brian up ahead of us, not wilty at all, looking as kingy and queeny as they possibly could.

"Dude, your dress is tripping me out." Mike pointed at me.

I glanced down, suddenly even more aware of my ridiculously stained dress. In the unflattering fluorescent lights of the restaurant, my dress was now very, *very* iridescent. Not lightly shimmery. Not subtly sparkly. I was freaking glowing. And when I shifted, the color rippled like water. The stains on my dress almost looked 3-D. I was a walking lava lamp. This was a nightmare. And the thought of Allyson, Grecian goddess flag twirler, glaring at my disaster of a dress was too much to handle. I felt sick.

"I gotta go to the bathroom," I said to Mike. "Get me a Combo Number Two. No meat!" I shoved my way through the crowd, linebacker style, hoping no one would stop me to talk. Fortunately, no one did, and I escaped to the large handicapped stall, where there was plenty of room to pace and think.

Is she after Ian? And where IS he?

The bathroom door opened. I heard the familiar sound of heels clicking against tile that reminded me of beautiful percussion instruments. I bent down and glanced under the stall door.

The hem of a white dress. Silver, strappy Jimmy Choo heels. Allyson.

Oh, no. Oh, lord. What was she doing? Her phone rang and it made me cringe . . . her ring tone . . . a Journey song. She was lucky it wasn't "Open Arms," or I'd have ripped hers off. Hers was "Don't Stop Believin'." Even her optimism was annoying.

All I could hear was her side of the conversation, but it was all I needed.

"Hey, you."

"I saw her a minute ago. She disappeared. But she's here. Mike and Other Mike brought her."

She's spying on me??

"Just two? Let's do more than that. Make this a real party, you know?"

"No problem—I'll meet you there."

"Wait, everyone's wondering where you are. You're taking a long time."

She's talking to Ian? They're meeting?!

"Totally, I understand. You know that. Brian's such a jerk."

What the—?

"If people keep calling and bugging you, then turn your phone off."

Turn it off ? Who else would be calling him?

"Just be careful, and look out for cops. That stuff's illegal, you know."

"You're welcome. You're always welcome. But I wouldn't do this for just anyone. You know that, right?"

Do WHAT for him?

[giggle]

Oh my god, she's giggling!

"See you in a few."

I peeked through the slender gap in the stall door and watched as she layered on gobs of pink, glittery lip gloss.

She had been talking to Ian. He was doing something illegal! They were going to meet! Is that lip gloss Bonne Bell Cherry Lip Smackers?!

My heart spun and buzzed around like a hummingbird. I pressed on my chest to slow it down.

She puckered her lips and gave herself an air kiss. "This will work," she said to Ugh.

I knew what the right tint of lip gloss could do to a guy. And so did she.

As soon as she was gone, I burst out of the bathroom and pushed through the crowd. Mike, Other Mike, and the girls were only a few people away from the cashier.

"What'd you say you wanted?" Bliss called out to me.

I couldn't answer. The tears were welling up and I couldn't be there anymore—definitely not under fast food fluorescent lights.

I rushed out to the parking lot and checked my phone. No call from him. He called *her*, not me. HER!

I paced around in the handicapped parking spot, talking to myself. "I will call him. Confront him. Right? It's the only way. I'll tell him I know he's trying to hook up with Allyson on our prom night. I'll tell him I know he's engaged in some type of illegal activity. I'll tell him to take this blue rose and shove it. Yes."

I came to a halt.

Suddenly the thought of listening to his voice—so soothing and reasonable—made me even angrier. I didn't want to be reasoned with. I wanted to yell! I wanted to grow twice my size, bust out of my dress with green skin, and terrorize neighborhoods. But yelling and Hulkifying myself was the last thing I should do.

Instead I called Hailey.

No hellos, she just went right in. "Buffy is about to kill her boyfriend because he's a sadistic killer! Is this important?!"

"Didn't you get my message?"

"Message? No, I was busy with Buffy prep!"

"Ian ditched me."

"What?"

"I'm stuck at In-N-Out with Mike and Other Mike and Serenity and Bliss and my dress is ripped and stained and sewn together with wire and now it's glowing like a lava lamp, and Ian is out doing favors probably for Allyson and I overhead her say he's doing something illegal. I hate Ian Clark!"

"Wait. You're with *The Mikes*?"

"And their dates. The Ledbetter girls. Who don't even go by names. Just their essences."

Hailey sighed. "And here I thought it was just the *Buffy* plotline that was messed up. Have you been sucking the crazy smoke?"

"This is a disaster."

"You tanked?"

"I gotta get out of here."

"Bent? You're bent!"

"Hailey, I don't even know what that means!"

"I'll come get you."

"No, you're in your jammies having a *Buffy* marathon. Licorice, too?"

"Out of it. Had to settle for mint chocolate chip ice cream."

"I'll get the Mikes to take me home. I'm sure they can drive me when they're done eating."

Hailey giggled at this. "Um, I don't think that's how it works. Partiers party, eat, and then usually the whole process starts all over again, sweetie. Just be careful, okay? I'll come get you if you want."

"I'm all right. You know what? Forget Ian. I'm gonna go back to crushing on—"

"Stop with the Anderson Cooper thing."

"He's reliable!" My phone beeped. I glanced at the screen . . . Ian. "I have to go. My phone . . . it's *him*!"

"Wow. That *is* reliable."

"Not Anderson. *Ian*!"

"I'm sure he has a reasonable explanation," she said in a rushed tone, knowing I needed to hang up. "Lots of people do normal illegal stuff that makes perfect sense. Go get him, sweetheart."

"Okay, okay, I'll call you later."

I quickly hung up and pressed the "accept new call" button, but it was too late; I had missed it. Just as I was about to call him back—*Bling!*—I received a new text.

It'd better be the truth—something reasonable. Not some lie about how he had to save some poor kitten with cancer stuck on a tightrope. Or whatever.

Meet me at Hampton Inn. I'm sorry. I'll explain. Your mother—

The text cut off. Another downside to owning a free phone from your cell phone carrier. You can only get texts less than sixty characters. How could anyone explain why he ditched his potential girlfriend at prom in sixty characters or less? He couldn't. And he had the nerve to bring *my mother* into this? Of all the heartstring tugging-tactics . . .

Even if I called him back and asked for the truth, he'd never come right out and admit he'd turned into Johnny Lawbreaker, lost track of time, and decided to call Allyson before he called me. There was no excuse that could make up for that.

The truth was, Ian had his mind on someone else's lip-glossed lips. Not mine.

How come it took me this long to realize all Ian Clark wanted from me was friendship? And nothing more.

I pushed the off button and watched the glowing screen fade away. Ian seemed to be doing the same thing—fading. I charged back into the restaurant and flopped into a seat next to the Mikes and the girls, who were sitting at a long table in uncomfortable hard, plastic chairs that didn't even swivel.

"The food's taking forever." Mike was making pictures out of the paper he tore off his straw. He was writing messages. *I heart you*, with an arrow pointing to Serenity. That girl was the proud owner of Mike's bleeding heart. It made my stomach ache. When would I be the one getting paper straw messages?

"Where's Ian?" Other Mike asked. We had talked about it in detail in the car, but he had been too busy trying to keep his balance on the coolers to remember.

"He's out doing favors," I reminded him in my I'm- trying-to-not-show-bitterness voice.

"Right now?" he asked. "Couldn't he help Grandma get her grocery shopping done some other time?" Other Mike was very talkative in the presence of In-N-Out burgers.

"Not that type of errand, I'm guessing."

He perked up. "Oh. Oh! Tell him to hook me up."

"Not that type either, I'm hoping." But I wasn't sure of anything anymore. Before I knew it, someone had slipped into the seat next to me.

"Can I sit here?" It was Brian Sontag. I shrugged. It's not like I was in charge of seating order.

"Sure."

But then it hit me: where there was Brian Sontag, there was—

"Hi." Allyson elegantly sat down in the seat across from us. "Having fun, Justina?"

I didn't respond. My eyes locked on the exit sign.

"Your dress looks good. What'd you use to tie it together? Fishing wire? Did Ian do that for you?"

I was used to her being sarcastic, but she sounded sincere, which totally confused me. Was this the calm before the hair pulling? Was she toying with me like Hannibal Lecter? I was *not* going down *Silence of the Lambs*–style with Allyson Moore getting into my psyche.

I supposed I could've been reasonable and assumed she was being genuinely nice. . . . But no, I was starving, so I assumed she was making plans to skin me alive in a basement.

But then again, that conversation in the bathroom was all the evidence I needed.

Serenity must have noticed I was not in the right state of mind to defend myself, so she stepped in. "I fixed her dress. She needed someone to *help* her."

Serenity stared Allyson down with an intense heat—the Ledbetter girl in her was starting to come out. She was about to go werewolf on her.

Brian tried to change the topic. "So where *is* Ian?" Which was not a good choice of topic. "Wait, he didn't dump you, did he?"

And suddenly I felt an instant jabbing pain in my right shin. "Ow!!!" Total immense pain!

Allyson looked under the table. "Oh my god! I'm so sorry!"

"You *kicked* me!!"

"I didn't mean to!"

Serenity jumped up, fist coiled, ready for action. "What the hell?"

"I swear!" Allyson pleaded, her arms flailing to protect her polished rock of a head. But it looked as though Serenity was about to kick some serious flag-twirling butt.

"That shin kick was meant for me." Brian stood up too, hands out, trying to stop the girl-on-girl hair pulling that was about to erupt.

"It's okay," I said to Serenity. She took in a deep breath and slowly sat back down, her eyes still squinty and full of protective rage.

Brian turned to me. "I'll get you some ice."

The pain was intense. I didn't want them to see me cry. I fake smiled and whimpered, "Just need some air."

Allyson leaned across the table, hands clasped as if she were a church choir member. "I just didn't want him to bring up Ian. Thinking about him might upset you."

"Me? Upset?" I don't know why I didn't confront her. Why didn't I tell her I knew she'd been talking to him? My voice cracked, and I said, "This has been the best night of my life."

With that, I jumped up and raced out to the parking lot, where I let out a hyena- like squeal. Those ridiculous Jimmy Choo pumps were lethal weapons. And she was aiming for Brian's leg? Right. She didn't want me to think about Ian because *she didn't want me to think about Ian!*

"Here, put this on it." Brian had joined me and handed over a bag of ice.

"Thanks." I plopped down on the curb and gently placed the ice on top of my new shin indentation, wincing from the pain.

"Sorry about that. It was my fault, really."

"You're not the one who kicked me."

"No, I was stupid. She said something earlier about making sure I didn't mention Ian to you."

"Did she say where he is?" I asked in disbelief. Allyson seemed to know where Ian was, and I had no clue. What in the parallel universe was going on?

"She said something about you getting upset if you found out where he went. I dunno—I can't remember exactly. I tune her out sometimes." He reached over and adjusted the ice pack on my shin. "Sorry I brought him up. I didn't mean for this to happen."

He ran his fingers through his short, buzzed hair, and his smell washed over me. Sweet. A little spicy. Maybe even a little minty. Nice.

"Brian?"

"Yeah?"

"Why do you think your date knows where my date is? Don't you think that's weird?"

He took a deep breath and puffed up his cheeks before letting the air out slowly. "Allyson seems to be friends with everyone. She likes to help people out. Sometimes too much. She has a problem with making other people's business her own."

If only she'd stay out of my business—maybe I wouldn't be crumpled on the pavement at the In-N-Out. I wiped my face, making sure there weren't any remaining tears, and handed him the ice pack. "I'm okay. The pain is only slightly unbearable now."

He helped me to my feet. It felt weird having Allyson Moore's boyfriend take care of me. But I wasn't going to complain. "Thanks," I said. "I seem to be finding help in surprising places tonight."

He smiled, and his eyes softened. His smell eased over me again. I had a weakness for boy smells—they made me say and do things I later regretted. So I quickly turned away to go back inside, but everyone was emptying out of the restaurant, full on greasy burgers. I peered around looking for the Mikes, hoping they would come out with my meatless burger wrapped in paper, all cozy and warm.

"We'll give you a ride." Allyson had walked up. "We're going to a party at the Hampton Inn. Come with us, 'kay?" She winced, like she felt sorry for me.

I wasn't about to be the third wheel in Allyson Moore's world. Especially at some party at a hotel. And especially not because she felt sorry for me. But then her words reverberated in my swirling, confused, food-deprived brain. "Wait. Did you say Hampton Inn?" Ian's text had said to meet him there. That's what Allyson was talk-ing to Ian about on her cell. *They* were planning to meet at the Hampton Inn.

"Yeah. Maybe Ian will be there?" She said it like a question, as if she didn't know.

My fist clenched. But punching out the prom queen in the parking lot of the In-N-Out was beyond redneck. Surely there was a glimmer of class left in me.

I decided to have her send him a message instead. "When you see Ian there, tell him I said I'm glad I gave the ring back."

"He gave you a ring?"

She didn't need to know I was referring to a two-dollar Shoney's vending machine daisy ring—she just needed to know it was a ring. "He'll know exactly what it means." I pushed my hair back in an exaggerated way, trying to look super casual.

"Just come to the hotel." She swallowed hard, clearly having a difficult time getting the pretend-nice words out. "Please, Justina."

I picked at my fingernail. "No."

Allyson threw her arms up in exasperation and headed out to the car without waiting for Brian.

"So you're not coming?" Brian shoved his hands into his pockets.

The last thing I needed was to hang out with another guy who was being nice and smelled good—Operation Lips Locked was still in effect. I pressed my lips together and shook my head.

Brian turned and followed Allyson to his car, where she was waiting with folded arms and judgmental eyes. Even her tennis balls looked a little deflated. While he held the door open for her, she yelled something at him. I could tell it was of the nasty sort, because he dropped his head. No wonder he tuned her out. Why couldn't Ian?

The Mikes and the girls skipped out of the building, arms locked, attached at the hips. Like human magnets.

"Got my no-meat burger?" I asked with my hand out, ready to scarf down all that cheese and bread, wrapping paper and all.

Other Mike's mouth fell open. "Dude . . . you were gone!"

"So you . . ." I was sure this was not what I wanted to hear.

"Ate it."

Mike punched him on the arm. "I told you that was for her, bro. Why'd you—"

"I was hungry." Other Mike placed his hands on my shoulders, "Sweetness"—he dipped his chin to his chest—"I am a horrible person."

"No. You're not." Luckily, the pain in my shin was overpowering the hunger pain in my stomach, and I was able to have a brief moment of empathy.

"Let's go!" Bliss held up a piece of paper, one she had ripped from the yellow pages. "Got the address. Four twenty- seven East Main."

"Let's do it!" Serenity threw her arms in the air, and the girls howled again. Their howling was amazing—it was in harmony.

I knew East Main was where the Olive Garden was. Thank god these partiers had *serious* munchies. Suddenly I didn't care one bit that we weren't going to go find Ian. He wasn't going to ditch me . . . I was ditching him.

After a few tries, the Caddy finally started and I bounced in my seat as I drove, because I had a killer case of the giddies. . . . I was on my way to a bowlful of pasta and endless bread sticks. Yum.

Yumyumyumyumyumyum.

With the promise of all those carbs, I managed to zip the Beast over to 427 East Main—seven blocks and four turns away—in under three minutes. We rolled into one of many empty parking spots. It was deserted and dark, and the only light came from one dim streetlamp and a flickering candle in a shop window.

This was no Olive Garden.

Chapter Eleven
CORN NUTS

"I NEED TO go to the bathroom," I say. Not because I need to go to the bathroom. I say it because this is the part where my story goes from pathetic to officially pathetic. And I want to run away.

Gilda hands me a key hanging off a metal rod and points over my head. "Back corner."

I cross the store with my head lowered and lock myself in yet another bathroom. There's a small mirror over the grimy sink. It's the kind of mirror that actually should be used for a metal toilet or something, because the reflection isn't real, it's distorted. Carnival-like.

Or maybe this is how I really look. A freak? A non-human?

I don't know the truth anymore. About anything. I can hear laughter coming from the store. Gilda and Donna. Laughing about my ridiculous life, I'm totally sure. I glance around, looking for some sort of window to the outside, and I imagine myself escaping, maybe like Harrison Ford, with a dagger clamped between my teeth. I'd much rather play Indiana Jones right now than go back out there to face them. Because this next part of my story, I don't want to tell—the part where I find out how he really feels about me.

I just wish I had heard it from you, Ian. It would have changed everything.

"You okay?" Gilda taps lightly on the door.

I turn on the faucet. "Yep. Be out in a sec." I splash water on my face and stare at my distorted reflection. "Tell them what happened," I say to myself. "Nothing is black and white. Tell them."

I slip out of the bathroom and ease myself back onto my stool while Gilda organizes the Reese's Miniatures display, and Donna digs into a bag of corn nuts.

"Want one?" Donna asks.

I nod, even though I'm not all that hungry anymore and I'd much rather have something from Gilda's Reese's display. Before I can even start explaining what happened next, Donna starts in with her advice. "Here's what I'm thinking." She crunches loudly. I start crunching loudly too, and she has to practically yell because we sound like dueling cement mixers. "This Allyson girl?"

"Yeah?" *Crunch.*

"She's a Parasite Pal."

"Parasite Pal?" *Crunch. Ow. Did I just break a tooth?*

"She's the type of girl who pretends to be your friend. And deep down she really does want to be your friend."

I pick at the igneous rock now lodged in my teeth. "I don't think so."

"She does. She's a parasite. Because she wants what you have."

Double-crunch. "A filthy blue dress?"

Donna shakes her head. "Captain Scumbag. Or at least someone *like* Captain Scumbag. Even if she doesn't get him, it gives her hope that a guy like that is real to *someone.* Does that make sense?"

She pauses this time. A real pause. She *actually* wants to know if this makes sense to me. I swallow hard. Because it does. It makes perfect sense.

"But you have to be careful: the moment they see a crack in the armor, they charge. She'll snag him when you're not looking."

I clutch my stomach. I have no idea where he is right now, and all I can do is hope it's not somewhere with her. Did I leave a crack open? Is she charging?

Donna shrugs and pops another nut in her mouth. "But as far as friends go"—*Crunch!*—"a Parasite Pal is not an awful one to have."

"Why?" I ask, because any phrase with the word *parasite* in it sounds like something one needs to quickly repel.

"She'll do anything for you. Give you anything you want. They're confusing. Some girls don't even know they have one."

I think of Eva being consoled by Brianna—who, of course, ended up in the back of a limo with Eva's date. Parasite Pal.

I nod. "But why doesn't Ian see she's trying to snag him?"

"Follow along, doll." She grips the side of the counter. "Men are scumbags. The definition of scumbag includes a Section B, which defines a scumbag as a man who enjoys having the parasite feed his ego—sucking his ego blood, so to speak." She scrunches her face. "Is this too graphic?"

It is too graphic and it also doesn't sound like Ian. Unless I'm missing something.

"It's . . . um . . . technical."

"I took a human psychology class at Fresno State. It's all science."

"What if he never figures it out? What if I've lost Ian to her?"

"He'll figure it out. But by the time he does, you'll be long gone. There's nothing you can do about it, doll. It's a biological survival instinct-type thing that allows our species to evolve." I was starting to question how much attention she'd paid in her psychology class. But she was on a roll. "And so the wrong people mate and then their kids are screwed up and they spend their lives in search of a perfect partner. But it never happens because the parasites move in first, so they hook up with the wrong person and the cycle starts all over again. It's how humans have survived all this time. We're motivated by unhappiness."

Gilda folds her arms. "You've had one too many corn nuts, Donna." She snatches the bag from her. "We're not going to depress the poor girl any more, okay?"

While I appreciate her stepping in at this point, I want to hear more of what Donna has to say. "But what about what Pastor Rick said? Maybe guys behave based on how they're treated by girls. Maybe I was the one who pushed Ian away."

"What are you saying?" Donna squeezes her eyes shut for a moment. "Of *course* you didn't—"

"No," I interrupt. "This next part . . ." I pause, feeling the rush of tears as they gather with a mob mentality and plot their return. "It's the part I don't want to tell you."

"Why, doll?"

"Because I found out how Ian really feels about me."

"Aww, honey," Gilda says. "We can't control if people fall in love with us. You're a beautiful girl. This will fade from memory soon."

My voice trembles. "But the words keep lingering in my head."

"What did he say to you?" Gilda asks.

"It wasn't him. I heard it from someone else."

"Parasite Pal," Donna offers.

"No, Allyson didn't tell me."

She squints her eyes. "Your BFFF?"

"It's BFF. Two F's. And no, it wasn't Hailey. It was a stranger."

"What stranger is this?" Gilda puts her hands on her hips like she's going to kick this stranger's butt.

"It was Fritz." I lift my arm so they can see. "The guy who gave me this tattoo."

Chapter Twelve
TINKER BELL TATTOO

I STARED AT the closed sign on the heavy wood doors of the Olive Garden. The staff was vacuuming and cleaning tables. I had no idea it was already almost midnight. All I could think about was noodles and marinara. And bread. And garlic. And—

"Come on." Serenity put her arm around me as she dragged me away from the restaurant, toward a creepy- looking shop next door. "We'll find you some nuts or something."

The Funky Monkey Tattoo Shop had a small wooden sign and was only noticeable because of the tie-dyed flag hanging outside the front door and a candle flickering in the darkened window. It was tucked in the corner of the strip mall next to a Relax The Back store. "We're going to a head shop?" I stood still, my sequoia tree feet rooted firmly in the asphalt.

"It's not super you know . . . *legal* to call it a head shop," Mike explained. "Sure, there may be people who consider themselves pot-heads who frequent the establishment, but we are not such people." He spoke loudly as he looked around, like a cop might pop out of the Michaels craft store. "The Funky Monkey is just a sticker and superfun happy store. That's all."

"Superfun happy!" the girls yelled, charging the door.

Mike led us inside, and the smell of incense, deep and woody, washed over me, causing an instant headache, the same kind I get when my mom goes crazy with the coriander; but then I get used to it. It was the same with this incense— within a moment I hardly even noticed it.

The hardwood floors were the only bare item in the store— the walls and ceiling were smothered with tapestries, posters, and beads. The air was dense. Thick.

"The Mikes!" A half man/half wooly mammoth with a long braided gray beard emerged from the back of the store. "'Bout time you dudes got down here. I was about to lock up." He stopped and looked us up and down. "Whoa. What the—"

"Prom." Mike spun around, all proud of himself but slightly off balance. "Check out the duds." He patted himself to make sure his buttons were buttoned and his fly was up. The guy side-hugged and fist-bumped Mike, then introduced himself to me.

"I'm Fritz." He stuck his Jolly Green Giant hand out. He was wearing a pink tie-dyed shirt, loose pants that looked suspiciously similar to pajamas, and no shoes on his pudgy feet. The long, gray, frizzy hair on his head looked like the source of how he got his name—like he'd been hit by lightning and . . . *Fritz!*

"Justina." I extended my hand, which disappeared inside his. "I'm . . . just . . . driving these guys around."

"No 'just' with these guys. Driving them around means having an *experience*."

I nodded. "True."

Fritz glanced around, adding up the numbers. We were obviously one person short.

His eyes landed on me. "No date?" Serenity stepped up and answered before I could.

"We're not talking about him. One of those off-limit things."

"It's okay. I can talk about it." I stiffened my posture. "Ian, my date, my so-called best friend, left me at the dance. He's doing something illegal. He keeps calling Allyson Moore on her cell phone. He's a jerk," I said, as if it were a mundane grocery list.

Fritz nodded slightly, like this was no unusual story to him, then turned to the Mikes. "What're you guys browsing for tonight?"

"The girls want tattoos." Mike tilted his head when he looked at me, like I was the goofy mascot. "I mean, Serenity and Bliss want tattoos. Justina has plenty of flair going on with that psychedelic dress of hers. And matching corsage." He shot me an I-feel-sorry-for-you-but-don't-want-to-say- it-type smile.

I smirked. He was being funny/sweet/supportive, but I wanted to chuck both the dress and the roses down a sewer drain.

Fritz slipped on his reading glasses and dug around behind the counter for tools. "What kind tonight, girls?"

They had clearly thought this through, because they both squealed, "Hearts!"

Fritz led the four of them through a beaded curtain behind the counter while I waited in the front of the store. Witnessing the drilling and the blood and the pain was not something my oh-so-empty stomach could handle. I could hear Bliss squeal and laugh as Fritz worked on her upper arm. She was handling the pain well. Maybe even liked it.

I had heard *that* rumor about Ledbetter girls, too.

Funny how no one at my school ever mentioned the part about Ledbetter girls being just plain awesome.

The store was pretty standard for a head shop, or I mean, a happy fun sticker shop. There was a counter full of hemp paper, hemp candles, hemp toilet paper, hemp, hemp, hemp. And then there was the pro selection of lava lamps. I mentally added the green and blue one to my Christmas wish list. But I was a little surprised by the separate counter area devoted completely to carvings of dragons and gargoyles.

Their carved faces were gothic and gnarly. Like how I feel without proper blood-sugar flow. *Man, I'm starving.*

Right next to the dragons was a rack full of clothes. They were all goth-looking shirts—black with skulls and flames. I spotted one perfect all-black girls sweater that would've made Hailey proud for its skintightness, and made me happy for its all blackness.

The price tag read $65.

Yikes. That would wipe out almost ten weeks of my clothing allotment.

Ian knew why I bought all my clothes secondhand, and even though I'd told him nearly every detail of my ridiculous life, I'd never gotten the nerve to tell him why I only bought black. I guess even as comfortable as he made me feel with his old clunker of a Mercedes and love of 7-Eleven nachos, it couldn't erase my embarrassment.

The truth was, the thrift store in our town rocked. Seriously rocked. The majority of the clothes were donated by girls from my high school. Correction . . . their *mothers* donated their clothes after they went through their daughters' closets and yanked out last year's designer clothes to make room for *this* year's designer clothes. Some people drove a long way to shop at the thrift store in my town. Oscar de la Renta for $4.99?!

But a few years ago I made the mistake of buying a Chanel print blouse on half-price orange-dot Tuesday for $1.99. Brianna Portman—sweetheart that she is—stopped me in the hall with a scowl on her face. "That's my shirt. My mom gave that away to charity. Why are *you* wearing it?"

I lied. I told her my mom had bought it at the mall and that I didn't know what she was talking about. But her eyes fell to the one little stain at the hem of the shirt—a sure indication I was a complete liar. And cheap.

So the day after Brianna confronted me about wearing her shirt, I only bought black. I used a black Sharpie marker to touch up any stains, and made sure there was nothing unusual about it—no ruffles, no prints, no intricate embroidery. No one could argue with that—a black shirt was a black shirt.

I don't think anyone ever caught on to my black Sharpie trick. I walked the halls of Huntington High wearing all their black hand-me-downs and they didn't have a clue. I guess everyone just thought I was dark and emotional.

And tonight, I definitely was. Because more than anything, I missed Ian.

There had to be an explanation. I needed to talk to him. I pushed the on button on my phone and when the display came up it said I had four voice mails.

My heart triple-flipped. The first one was from my mom. Annoyed, I fast-forwarded through it, and the next one was from Ian. He had been trying to call me!

—*Running a little late. Where are you?*

—*Still trying to get there. Don't be mad. Get a snack.*

—*Oh man. Can you turn your phone on, Justina??*

I listened to the messages, hoping to get an explanation, but no, they were worthless. Just his soothing, even voice trying to smooth it all out—as if I were some "buddy" he might catch up with at a party later.

I just wanted him to be honest. Was that too much to ask? Did he think I couldn't handle knowing he was selling drugs or making meth or burying bodies or whatever illegal stuff he was into?

I had to know what was going on. We needed to talk.

I hit 2 on my speed dial, but immediately it went to voice mail. None of this made sense. Why wasn't his phone on? Had he taken Allyson's advice? How could he make me believe he was a handle-first type of guy—for months!—and then in one night become someone else completely?

Baffling.

I decided I'd better listen to Mom's message. It was on the worthless side, too.

—*Just got home from the fundraiser. There was a little problem when I got home but I've figured it out. Don't worry about me . . . I didn't want you to think I was getting too involved again. That's why I didn't bother you with it. You'll be home by two, right? Did everyone love your shoes? I knew they would!*

No, Mom. They didn't all love my shoes.

And why would she call me with some household problem? It was *my* prom. I couldn't fix a toaster or whatever from the dance floor! Not that I had danced with anyone. Not intentionally, anyway.

But at least she'd figured it out on her own.

My mind drifted back to Ian. This was exactly the type of thing I'd talk to him about—my well-intentioned, overbearing mother figured out her own problem.

But I couldn't talk to him—for some reason his phone was off. It didn't feel like I'd ever get closer to the truth.

"I love it!" Serenity yelled from the back room.

Through the beaded curtain I could make out the silhouette of her and Mike in the far corner. Hugging. Swaying. Him gazing at her new tattoo, her gently resting her head on his shoulder.

Them—ridiculously sweet. Me—totally jealous. I had imagined Ian and me standing just like that right before we kissed. But he had been willing to give that up for a flag twirler who told stories with dramatic hand gestures. Maybe Allyson was more interesting. Maybe he liked that she'd joined the flag corps. That she was the head of the prom committee, as embarrassing as that would be. That she had a Journey song for her ring tone—by choice, not force. And that she didn't care what anyone thought about any of it. She did what she wanted. No worries.

She wasn't like me at all.

I pushed my way through the beaded curtain. "I want a tattoo."

"What?!" Serenity herded me over to the corner for a quick lecture. "I know Ian's being a jerk and all, and lord knows I've made life-altering decisions in the name of rage, but do you really want to do this? Be rational, okay? Eat some peanuts."

Her argument was understandable, but for the first time that night, my mind felt clutter-free. "I'm not doing this because

I'm mad. I want to do something without worrying about the consequences."

She nodded. "Okay, okay. That's solid." She gave me a quick hug. "Just making sure you have a clear head." She guided me by the shoulders and led me into the chair opposite Fritz.

He was on a stool next to a bright work light, cleaning needles. Gulp.

Serenity clamped down on my shoulder. "Want me to stay with you?"

The Mikes were out in the store playing air guitar to Led Zeppelin, making Bliss giggle almost to the point of hysteria. "No, you go hang with them. I can do this."

She waved sweetly as she pushed her way through the beaded curtain, and I was alone with Fritz. He continued to clean his tools. He whistled. He did not talk.

"So, can you show me some pictures or something?" My toes bounced, eyes darted, nerves rattled.

Fritz glanced at me over his glasses.

"Of tattoos," I added. "Some choices?"

"So *you* want to be the risk taker tonight, huh?" He crossed his legs in a deliberate fashion, as if he wasn't so convinced.

"I need to take a risk. And I need to stop caring."

"So which is it? You need to take risks? Or you need to stop caring?"

"It all sounds good to me. Can't I do both?" I pushed down on my knees to get my toes to stop bouncing.

He shrugged and motioned to my stomach, which was grumbling loudly. "They're *your* needs."

True, maybe all I needed was a veggie burger. But I knew I needed Ian, too.

At least his friendship. That was one thing I couldn't bear to lose.

Ian was the guy who would call to check in on me three days before my period normal for a girl to curl up in bed with a hot water bottle. One day, he finally realized I didn't need his emotional support, I just needed licorice and Motrin.

But what I loved most about our friendship was the way he said my name . . . always dripping with adoration. And annoyance. I had always figured that's what had drawn Ian to me. My adorably low tolerance for PMS mixed with my annoying all-black wardrobe. It was sexy to him.

Probably.

"Give me a tattoo." The words came out, but then my heart did that jumping thing and my head did that annoying weighing-of-consequences thing. Ugh. "But don't give me a real one," I blurted.

"You worried about what other people will think?"

I lowered my head. "Always."

Fritz flashed me a smile, though it was barely visible behind his wooly beard. "Wasn't planning on it. It's my policy to never drill on people who haven't eaten. Hungry people make bad decisions." He pulled a drawer wide open. "Pick one."

There were lots of choices. Hearts. Lions. Disney characters. "That one," I said, pointing to a punk Tinker Bell with ripped wings and fishnets and combat boots. She was the spitting image of me. She was supposed to be sweet and beautiful, but she was ripped and torn. All I needed were combat boots. Which would have been an improvement over these shoes.

"Nice choice." Fritz pulled out a towel, a bowl of water, and a damp sponge. It didn't take long, but he did have to press pretty hard.

I can't say it was painless.

While he worked his magic, I explained everything to him. How Ian and I met, how he handed me the bat handle first, how he brought me the licorice and Motrin when I was on my period, how he wore that green shirt, how we flirted and dipped our toes in the water but never plunged. And then I told him how Ian ditched me, and about Allyson.

He shook his head. But didn't say anything.

"What?" I asked.

Fritz put his tools away. "Sounds like you don't have all the pieces to this puzzle."

"Like?"

He shrugged. "All I know is the best buds come straight from the plant. The source. Not from some guy on Lexington Avenue selling it to you in a dirty Ziploc. If you want to know how he really feels about you, you gotta go to the source."

"Lexington Avenue?"

He tilted his head down, looking at me over his glasses, and blinked heavily.

"You mean Allyson? I'm not about to waste one second talking to that—"

He raised his hand, stopping me. "Ian."

"But all I seem to be getting are excuses—"

"I don't think he'd go from being a handle-first kind of guy to a ditcher in one night. Find the puzzle piece. Go to the source."

I breathed in deeply. "You sound like one of those ninja wise men."

He pointed behind him to a display of bumper stickers. One read: go to the source. "Instant wisdom," he said, "for only a $1.29."

"Thanks, Fritz."

When the tattoo was dry, I joined the girls and the Mikes in the poster section, where the guys were discussing whether one of the skeletons in the posters was *actually* speaking to them.

Serenity and Bliss ran over to check out my new tat. I couldn't bring myself to tell them it was only temporary. They'd know I was a poser. A fake risk taker. A loser in all caps.

But Bliss grabbed my arm. "Oh my gosh!" She covered her mouth, then said, "Serenity, this is the best!"

Serenity rubbed my arm gently. "It rocks, Sweetness."

"Aren't you guys gonna make fun of me? It's not a real one."

She pulled up her strap to the side and pointed to her heart. "Temporary." She threw her arms in the air. "We're not *that* stupid."

I smiled. "Solid."

Just before we left, my eye caught something in a display sitting on the countertop. Silver and shiny. A ring.

A huge Muppet-looking daisy ring, two fingers wide.

Ohmygosh, ohmygosh.

Fritz stepped up to the counter. "Like it?"

"Yeah." My fingers shook as I flipped over the tag. It read:

Handmade, one of a kind...for someone special. $350

My stomach plummeted to the floor. Oh. My. Sweet. God. I had no idea.

"Some guy bought that ring a few weeks ago." Fritz shrugged and sipped on a Capri Sun. "But he returned it the next day."

I whipped my head up at him. "Did he say why?"

"Said his girlfriend was too worried people would make fun of it." He looked at me and raised an eyebrow. "He was pretty choked up about it. Why would his girlfriend care that much about what other people think?"

Fritz slid the ring on my finger. It fit perfectly. My eyes filled with tears—I couldn't hold them back. My words sputtered out. "He called me his girlfriend?"

Fritz nodded. "Did we just find a piece of the puzzle?"

I wiped my face. "Yeah. We did." Without a moment of hesitation, I pulled out the credit card Mom gave me for thrift store shopping and placed it on the counter. I knew Mom would read my statement and see how much I'd spent—an entire year's allowance.

But Ian Clark had called me his girlfriend. In public. At a head shop!

I finally knew how he felt—and it was before he had ever even kissed me. Apparently he didn't need to know how I kissed to seal the deal—he had tried to seal it with this ring. And I wouldn't accept it. I pushed it away . . . pushed *him* away. That's what this was all about.

Me.

Fritz rung me up and said, "Here's the box. . . ."

I shook my head. "I'll wear it out." My voice cracked. "Thank you, Fritz." I studied the ring again, knowing I would never take it off. Well, maybe for showers . . . Oh, what the heck—no, I would never take it off.

My eyes wandered to my royal blue watch. One a.m. "Oh my god."

"What's wrong?" Serenity spun me around.

"It's so late. I have to find him. We have to go!" I grabbed her by the arm and dragged her out toward the parking lot, the Mikes and Bliss following—adorable magnets that they were.

We all piled into the Cadillac, which didn't take long because I practically shoved them in while apologizing for groping them, but we had to go! I gunned it out of the parking lot, making the tires squeal. I was hell-bent. And yeah, totally crazy crackers.

"Where are we going?" Mike gripped the door handle for balance.

"To a party." My hands tightened around the steering wheel because I was determined to get there fast. And also to keep Beast from drifting.

"Right on," Mike said. "Which one?"

"The Hampton Inn." I turned to him, my face flushed. "I have needs."

"That's right, sister." He slid his beer over to me.

"Not that kind." The wind swirled around my head, and I sensed the remote pings of an unfamiliar feeling: hope. "I need to get to that party." I clenched my jaw. "I need to find out if I'm still his girlfriend."

Chapter Thirteen
NACHO CHEESE

"CAN WE PUT on a different song?" I ask, sounding like I'm trying to change the subject—which I am—but the singer is wailing lyrics like, "We were always meant to say good-bye."

Gilda doesn't even argue, and runs over to turn off the song.

Donna folds her arms and gets back to the topic at hand. "It's a *sticker*?"

"No, it's a temporary tattoo that eventually rubs off. He said it'll last for almost five days."

"A sticker."

I sigh and rub the tattoo gently, careful not to peel it off. I'm sure Gilda is trying to find something instrumental. She probably senses that song lyrics might send me spiraling.

"And you're in pain. Did you say *pain*?" Donna cocks her head to the side.

"He pressed down really hard with that sponge. Fritz is very thorough." She's not impressed with my Tinker Bell. *I'm* not even impressed. And it's not like Ian will ever see it. This thing will disappear after one shower, I'm sure.

But he would've been proud of me. I totally had the intention of getting a real tattoo. Intentions count, right?

If only I knew what yours were, Ian.

The speakers are now blaring soft jazz, and Gilda jogs back, clapping her hands like she's starting a cheer. "Let's focus on the important stuff, Donna. Ian wants her to be his girlfriend. This is fantastic!"

Donna pauses, unsure how fantastic this is, then finally says, "I have to admit, this is an interesting turn of events. Captain Scumbag seems to be a complicated fellow."

I bite my tongue, contemplating whether to tell her about his collection of snow globes. She wouldn't find him complicated . . . she'd find him baffling. And so do I.

The bell rings, and an elderly man shuffles up to the counter. He carefully pulls a fifty-dollar bill from his ancient, cracked wallet, which is stuffed to the max with pictures of what I assume are his grandkids. He's dressed in his Sunday best, red bow tie and all. He clears his throat and looks at Gilda. "Twenty on pump two and a fifth of whiskey." He turns to Donna and shoots her a wink. "Football all afternoon right after church." He snatches the bag of liquor and nods at Gilda. "Gotta get fueled up."

The old man scuffles off, but stops and turns back, quickly surveying the three of us, clearly sitting around not going anywhere. "Mind if I ask whatcha'll are talking about?" He looks directly at my dress. I can't blame him. I'd wonder too.

The three of us glance at each other and pause, wondering if we should tell him what we're discussing. But this story has gotten so long. And complicated. He wouldn't want to hear this—not exactly something to tell the grandkids.

But he's still standing there, getting older by the second, wanting to know. We all answer at the same time.

Me: The weather

Gilda: Politics

Donna: Scumbags

He nods, then shuffles along his way. He turns back one more time. "Stay away from the scumbags." He grabs his paper bag tight. "We're a hell of a lot of fun. But we're no good."

We watch in silence as he slips into his red convertible Camaro. It takes him three tries to time the clutch just right, then he peels away.

I kind of wish I had told him what happened. Maybe I need another male's perspective. But then again that sports car tells me he's going through a late-in-life crisis. Donna sighs again as she watches him leave. . . . her cougar status may not be as truthful as she says.

Gilda clears her throat, getting us back on track. "Can I point out the obvious?"

I flinch. "Yeah?"

"You spent $350 on a ring at a tattoo shop."

I nod.

"Your mother will read your credit card statement."

I nod again.

"Did you weigh the consequences of *that*?"

I shake my head. "No. And it felt good." I glance up at the nacho bar, knowing that if Ian were here he'd be creating an intricate multilayered nacho entrée to congratulate me on finally not worrying about what other people think.

It just never occurred to me that I'd be standing in this very 7-Eleven looking at the nacho bar without him next to me—bouncing on his toes as he placed jalapeños in their perfect spot.

Gilda coughs to get my attention. "So you found Ian and showed him the ring?

"It wasn't that easy. We got . . . delayed."

Donna shakes her head. "Damned drug pushers. They have no sense of time."

"It wasn't them. It was me."

Gilda rubs the back of her neck. "But why? You were so determined, right?"

"Look, I had no idea I'd have to deal with that police officer, much less that guy at the hotel who was stripped down to his underwear wearing a motorcycle helmet. I mean, it just took some time to get to the Hampton Inn. I tried, I really did."

Their mouths drop. I look down at my hands resting on my dress. "Let me back up a little. We were on our way to the hotel—"

Before I can continue, I realize I need some more nourishment. And without a thought, I walk over to the nacho cheese bar, remembering how many times I've watched Ian stand in this exact spot. I lift the ladle to the nacho cheese, dying for a taste after all those times of turning Ian down. "Can I?"

Gilda nods. And I scoop some into a plastic cup, dip my finger in, and taste.

It slides down my throat like heaven on a waterslide. So. Freaking. Delicious. Oh, man. Why didn't I let Ian buy me nachos? He knew how good they were, that's why he offered week after week, probably hoping someday I'd come to my senses and take it. I have deprived myself and I am an idiot.

"Did you get another stain at this party?" Donna interrupts my little nacho moment.

"No."

"A bruise?"

I shake my head.

"A rip?"

"No. I didn't *get* anything." I set the cup of nacho cheese down and lift my hand up for them to see—my ring finger. Bare as can be. "I lost something."

CHAPTER FOURTEEN

A ONE-OF-A-KIND MUPPET-LOOKING DAISY RING, $350

"YOU DIDN'T YELL *duck*!" Mike was completely wigging out. But I wasn't exactly experienced in the art of evading the police. In fact, there was something about those red-and-blue lights that intimidated me, and I'd instantly fold.

I was hauling it down Main Street, and we (unknowingly) passed a cop sitting in the parking lot of the Circle K, which, by the way, sucks. I would never bother going inside a Circle K. No magazine aisle? Really?

"We're screwed!" Mike was twisted backward in his seat, his eyes glued on the flashing lights.

"Sorry. I'm sorry!" I turned on my signal and started guiding Beast to the side of the road. Of course I had to manually lift the turn signal—*up, down, up, down*—it wouldn't do it without my help.

I pulled over into the gravel on the side of the road, not leaving much room for the approaching big, bad officer, who was, no doubt, going to be 6'10" and have flaming grenades for eyeballs. We were a bunch of prom party rejects sitting on coolers that were probably full of beer. We were going to jail. We were going to die. We were going to be on the news.

"Crap!" Mike was quickly stuffing plastic bags under his seat like he was playing a carnival game. "I don't know what's in these bags, but knowing my bro. . . we're in trouble."

Even though my usual motto was *Avoid Confrontation At All Costs*, my mind was focused solely on my new motto: *Find Ian Clark*. Plus, I was still the best friend of the girl who played kung fu with her words and talked her way out of everything.

I was no Hailey—but I *did* pay attention.

"We're not getting busted." I reached out and grabbed Mike's hand. "I can handle this. No worries, okay?"

He pressed his lips together tightly, not seeming convinced at all.

I glanced in the cracked side-view mirror. Officer Intimidation was approaching, flashlight drawn.

"Serenity?" I connected looks with her in the rearview mirror.

"Yeah?"

"Follow my lead."

She giggled. "Lead on, sweetheart."

The officer tapped on the window, and I rolled it down, which wasn't easy; it took both hands to crank it.

"Good evening, young lady." The officer had wire-rim glasses, a mess of pumpkin-pie orange hair, and very smooth, fair skin. He was practically a toddler. Was he even legal drinking age?

He peered into the back window. Serenity waved at him, so he half waved in response, then quickly stuck his hands on his hips. "Do you realize there is no seat back there?" Before I could answer, he followed up with, "And there are no seat belts." He cleared his throat. "Seats. And seat belts. They're both laws, kids."

He certainly was emphasizing the fact that we were kids, trying to deflect the fact that he had been one himself about three weeks ago.

I was about to deploy my Get-Out-of-Everything-à-la-Hailey tactic, but Mike leaned across the seat, getting a better look at Officer Toddler. "Dude! Do I know you?"

The officer lowered his head and glared at Mike. Then he cleared his throat again—which must be his signature technique for turning into Pretend Man. "No, don't think so."

"Wait!" Mike leaned in farther. "You graduated with my brother Jed. Class of '08. Aren't you Andy Brazeer?"

Oh my god, no wonder this guy became a cop. The horror of growing up with the name *Brazeer*! Poor guy.

He pushed his glasses up his nose. "*Andrew* Brazeer. Sure, I remember Jed. How's he getting along these days? Still crashing your parents' cars?" He snickered, obviously remembering some wild smash-'em-up high school memory.

"He crashes derby cars now, man."

Officer Andy looked over our Caddy. "But you can't *drive* a derby car, son. Not on regular roads, I mean."

At first I thought Mike might be getting somewhere with his don't-you-remember-my-brother plan, but things were going south again. Andy had called him *son*.

I needed to take control, so I put Hailey's tactic into effect.

Roll and deflect.

I gently pushed Mike back over to his side of the car, while looking up at the officer with big eyes—huge, moony, manga-style eyes with a dash of sparkle. "I understand if you need to ticket us, Andy. I mean Officer Brazeer. But . . . well . . . oh my gosh, this is so embarrassing. . . ."

He tapped his fingers impatiently on his flashlight. "Go on."

"My friend in the back?" I pointed behind me to Serenity. "She just got her"—I leaned out the window and whispered rather loudly—"her period. A *bad* one, sir."

Serenity hunched over and started moaning. That girl knew how to follow.

"It's prom night. And we have no protection. If we don't get a tampon or a maxi-pad—"

"Stop!" He held his hand up, looking like he was going to vomit.

Bingo. Males cannot handle tampon talk. Their automatic regurgitation reflex kicks in at the mere mention of sanitation products.

As women, it's the only weapon we have. That, and pepper spray. And boobs, Hailey would say.

I pushed on. "Do you know of a drugstore nearby, sir? Sir?!"

"I . . . I—" Officer Andy's face was quickly darkening, nearing pomegranate.

Serenity leaned up next to my face and tilted her head at the officer. "I need to get to my house. Quick! It's *gushing*!"

"Okay, okay. Don't panic!" He crouched down in the catcher's position, like she was about to give birth. "I'll get you somewhere safe. Where do you live? I'll escort you."

Crap. That's the last thing we needed—a police officer escorting us home. I couldn't waste any more time. I needed to get to Ian!

"The Hampton Inn," Serenity said.

I cocked my head at her, like she was lost.

Officer Andy quickly straightened back up, erect like a meerkat, and cocked his head at her, too. "What?"

"My mom, she's the night manager there. She always has tampons and maxi-pads and stuff for the customers. She's really good at her job. Can you take us there?" Oh, this girl was good. But the officer hesitated. Serenity looked down at her lap. "Oh, no."

He dropped back down to the catcher's position. "Okay! Stay close. I'll get you to the Hampton Inn right away." He hustled back to his patrol car, but just before he reached the door, he jogged back up to my window. "You said Hampton Inn, right? West side of Highway 5?"

I had no idea. "Yes! Hurry!"

As we pulled away from the curb, following closely behind Officer Brazeer, Mike leaned over and bonked me lightly on the head. "You're the best, Sweetness."

We pulled into the parking lot of the Hampton Inn and waved at Officer Andy as he drove away. It looked like the regular color had come back to his face. He waved back at us, even giving us a friendly toot on the police siren as he drove away. For a toddler, he was a very helpful man.

Bliss and Serenity howled and giggled while I found a parking spot. The Hampton Inn turned out to be not such a super-classy place. The sign outside read $49/night. Free change of sheets.

I had to park in a spot out in the far corner because the lot was almost full. Screams and howls came from the second floor as soon as we opened our door. Well, as soon as Mike opened *his* door and let me crawl out.

"Lez party! Oooowwwww-ooooo!" someone screamed from the balcony. A group of people leaned over to get a look at us, and when the Mikes gave them a thumbs-up they all exchanged howls. The balcony people raised their red plastic beer cups and they all howled some more.

Prom really brought out the werewolf in these people.

The Mikes plus Bliss and Serenity ran off to join the party while I locked the car doors and then double-checked them. Which seemed ridiculous since there were two windows missing.

Some habits are hard to break.

I looked down at my daisy ring and said to myself, "You are his girlfriend," trying to convince myself it was true. It felt odd to say the words. But exhilarating. I couldn't believe this was happening. I had found boyfriend material. And he felt the same way.

And that's when I heard the rumbling.

The rattling, clanging sound of Ian's old Mercedes. I stood on my tiptoes and saw his car coming down the street. My heart danced the hula, and tears—*happy* tears—filled my eyes. I'd found him!

I quickly applied lip gloss and prepared my best sweet, seductive look as I waited for him to turn in, but . . . wait. He wasn't slowing down. He kept going. He totally missed the turn—he was driving *past* the hotel!

Waving my arms, I broke into a sprint, my unmaneuverable high heels clopping against the pavement. "Stop! Ian!"

The drunkards on the balcony started mimicking me. "Stop, Ian, stop! I love you!"

I darted between cars, trying to get to the exit, while I screamed, "Wait, Ian! WAIT!!"

But over the clanging of his engine and the howls of the party, he couldn't hear me.

He was gone.

Where the hell was he going?!

I ripped the corsage off my dress and threw it toward his car—hoping to get his attention, but the corsage didn't go but ten feet. And landed in the gutter.

His taillights got smaller and smaller in the distance.

I felt like crawling into that gutter. And spending the rest of my existence as Gutter Girl.

But, no. No, no, no. I couldn't go live in a gutter—I had to make this right. Ian was worth the chase. Which meant I needed to go into that party and drag out my adorable human magnets so we could find him.

Operation Un-Locking Lips was in full effect.

There were people scattered all around the hotel, in the stairwell and hallways. Beer cups passed through hands and sloshed around to places it shouldn't, leaving puddles on the floor.

As I reached the door, I stepped over two girls sitting in the hallway. I didn't recognize them, but they looked gorgeous in their matching red dresses. They were staring at each other, holding hands, looking very much in love. I clenched my stomach. Seeing couples madly in love only reminded me that I *had* to find Ian. Soon.

As I entered the room, I immediately started coughing because of the thick smoke haze. The Mikes were out on the balcony with Serenity and Bliss, and I tried to squeeze myself past people to get to them.

"Where you headed, gorgeous?"

A tall guy wearing tuxedo pants and nothing else was sipping a beer and swaying as he waited for my answer.

"Trying to find my friends!" I yelled over the music, glancing around the room to find Allyson. I figured if she wasn't here either, I'd have my answer as to where Ian had gone.

But nothing. She wasn't anywhere to be found. Was she with him? My heart thumped double time. My fists clenched all on their own—my body was on autopilot. And it wanted to strangle.

"Strangle what?" The drunk guy asked.

I didn't realize I'd said it out loud. "Ha," I said. "Um, not strangle. I said . . . *strangers*. There are a lot of people here I don't know."

And sure enough, as I glanced over at the balcony, I realized I didn't recognize anyone around me. No Allyson. No Brianna. No one from Huntington High at all.

Wait. Was this the wrong party?

"What'd you say?" He was confused by me. The guy leaned down toward me so he could hear better, but he was clearly unaware of the concept of gravity as it relates to angles of beer cups. He poured half his Budweiser down the front of my dress.

"I'm sorry!" He laughed, but still managed to seem sincere. "Here, lemme clean you up."

He didn't bother to grab a towel, and he wasn't wearing a shirt, so he reached out to wipe me down—with his bare hands! It was possible he copped a feel (I wasn't sure . . . my Miracle Bra was ultra-padded) before I pushed his hands away.

"It's okay. I don't need help." I lifted his chin so he'd concentrate on my words. "What party is this?"

He raised his hands in the air, spilling the rest of his beer on his head. "The best party in the world, gorgeous!" And then he howled, of course.

"No, I mean what school?"

"Ledbetter. Go Wolves! Hey, aren't you in my geometry class?"

No wonder there was so much howling going on around here.

Then Officer Andy's question popped into my head. The Hampton Inn *west*? But it didn't make sense—why did Ian drive right by it?

"Wait, are there *two* Hampton Inns?"

"Sure," drunk guy said. "But the one on the east side of the highway sucks. Don't go there. It's attached to a Big Boy, but it closes at midnight. Plus those Huntington High jerks are partying over there. You should stay here—the west is the best—we're attached to an IHOP. Open twenty- four hours, baby!"

Oh good god, leave it to this ridiculous town to have the same hotel on both sides of the highway.

He leaned into me, almost falling over my feet. "Hey, wanna go get some pancakes?"

Of course I did.

But I had to get to Ian. That was why he drove right past me—he was going to the *east*-side Hampton Inn. He may have called her at the In-N-Out Burger, but he was looking for *me*, not Allyson.

I told my new drunk friend I'd go get him a refill, and pushed my way out to the balcony. The Mikes were deep in conversation with a guy holding a four-foot beer glass. Serenity and Bliss were gone.

Ugh. When will the Gods of Simplicity take over? "Mike, where are the girls? We have to go!"

"We just got here."

"This is the wrong party."

"No, repeat after me." Mike scrunched his eyebrows, looking very determined. "The motto is: *any* party is the right party."

"No." I put my hands on his shoulders, hoping he would concentrate on the importance of the words I was about to say. "The right party is the one Ian's at. The Hampton Inn. *East*."

"There're two?"

I nodded. "And there's a Big Boy attached." I didn't mention it would be closed, but we could make amends later.

"Let's get another party started!"

The Mikes waited for me while I searched for Serenity and Bliss. Luckily, it wasn't hard to find them; they were in the bathroom singing into their lipsticks.

"We have to go," I said. "We're at the wrong party."

"This party is bitchin'!" Bliss yelled as she pumped her fist in the air. "Didn't you see the guy running around in his underwear?"

"Which one? Not many people are fully dressed out there."

"The one wearing a motorcycle helmet. The Barracuda!" she yelped.

"Who?"

Serenity gracefully dropped her lipstick into her purse and calmly explained. "Frankie Aruda. We call him The Barracuda. He's a loon, man . . . gets crazy cash from the government. He's my biology lab partner."

Bliss threw her hands in the air. "Barracuuuuda!!"

Serenity moved in closer to me. "Every once in a while the Barracuda stops taking his meds and gets drunk enough to feel the need to strip down to his motorcycle helmet and tighty-whities. Bliss looks forward to this event."

"Huh." I wasn't really sure how else to respond. Normally I would fold and stay at a party I didn't want to stay at just to avoid a problem, but I was done being Miss Accommodating.

"I'm leaving," I said.

Serenity looked at me, a slow smile growing across her face.

"I have to find Ian. He's looking for me." I glanced at myself in the mirror, stained and wretched. "He's going to be disappointed, though."

Serenity pulled a brush out of her insanely large purse and combed my hair until it shined. "Let's go." She smacked me on the butt and nudged me out the door.

But as soon as we opened it, we were overtaken by the sights and sounds of the Barracuda. He was wearing only a motorcycle

helmet and tighty-whities, just like Serenity said, and he was on top
of a table, dancing.

Earlier in the evening, I hadn't quite understood Bliss' fascina-
tion with male anatomy and stir-fry vegetables. But when my eyes
drifted down . . . Oh. My. God.

I suddenly forgot why we were leaving. My cinder-block feet
were planted. I couldn't move. Bliss was so happy she was shivering.

"Let's go!" Serenity yelled.

But we were frozen. A combination of disbelief and pure, unbri-
dled state-fair-winning-junk curiosity.

"Look away!" Serenity grabbed us both by the shoulders. "We're
leaving. Justina is going to find Ian," she explained, like we were
toddlers. "We are all going to find him. Now march!"

And my group of the world's best refrigerator magnets escorted
me out to the car.

As we pulled out of the parking lot, the Mikes and the girls
leaned out their windows and howled back at their balcony friends.
They seemed determined to have fun whether they were coming or
going.

When we got to the east-side Hampton Inn, it was déjà vu.
More screaming from the second-floor balcony. Only this time they
weren't howling, they were barking. (We are the Huntington High
Bulldogs.)

And just like on the west side, the Mikes and their dates skipped
into the party while I stayed behind to lock the car. And unbeliev-
ably, I heard it again: the rumbling diesel engine of Ian's Mercedes.
I got up on my tiptoes and saw him backing out of a spot on the far
side of the parking lot.

He was leaving! "Ian, no!"

I ran across the lot, screaming his name, waving my arms, looking like a complete loon who gets crazy cash from the government.

He took a left and squealed out. Was he going back to the *other*
Hampton Inn?

Oh no, this can't be happening again. No, no, no!

The heel of my shoe stuck in the grass of one of the medians, causing me to fall into a pitiful heap on the ground. My body crumpled like I was covered with a wet blanket.

As my limbs became useless, my purse splattered to the ground, and out popped my cell phone, flipping and somersaulting and landing just on the edge of a sewer drain. I flopped over on my stomach and lunged at it, but—*tink, clink.* Gone.

My only way to communicate with Ian was now at the bottom of a sewer drain. And his car lights were getting smaller and smaller in the distance.

I needed something to throw at his car, anything to catch his attention and make him turn around!

In an act of desperation—*extreme* desperation, I'm fully aware— I reached for the one and only thing I could to use as a projectile. I tore the daisy ring from my finger, took aim, and launched it at his car. And missed by a good fifty feet.

The ring hit the pavement. But I had no idea where.

I wandered aimlessly between cars, bending down to look under wheels while I murmured angrily to myself.

Stupid. Stupid! What is wrong with me?! He told me to meet him here, so I went to a tattoo parlor?! And why the hell did I throw my ring at him?! I couldn't have thrown a shoe? These dumb, tanker-sized things are still on my feet and I didn't think to throw them instead?! And now it's an hour past my curfew and...wait... ANHOURPASTMYCURFEW?!

All I could do was hope that Mom was in a deep sleep, because I knew there'd be no way I could get the girls and the Mikes out of this party any time soon. Given the amount of beer that was sitting on that balcony, this was going to be a party they would dedicate some time to.

The Gods of Extreme Complication had clearly taken over my case.

Ian was gone. My phone was gone. My ring was gone. I was wandering in the Hampton Inn parking lot murmuring to myself, so clearly my dignity was gone, too.

Didn't he know I would be looking for him?

No. No, no, no.

I'm coming to find you, Ian.

Luckily, I found Serenity sitting on a love seat in the corner of the hotel room, oblivious to the mass of drunken people around her, pushing buttons on her phone.

"Here are the car keys. I'm not staying."

But she was busy, and only said, "Mmm-hmm."

"I'm going to go find Ian. I'm going to walk if I have to. I will wander the streets forever." Still no response. "Like Caine. In *Kung Fu.*"

Still nothing, so I gave up and scooched next to her. "What are you doing?"

"Talking to Mike."

"Where is he? Did he leave?"

She shook her head. "Over by the keg."

"Then why don't you just walk over there?" I glanced up, and sure enough Mike was pushing buttons on his phone.

"He's adorable. Look at this one."

I looked away—there was no way I could read adorable texts at that moment. "Seriously. I'm leaving." I jingled then dropped the keys next to her to make sure I got her attention.

"No you're not. We're here to find Ian." She looked up from her phone and glanced around the room. "Where is he?"

"He left. Squealed out of the parking lot right as we came in," I said, in a pretend-happy voice. "He must be going back to the other Hampton Inn. He's looking for me and we keep missing each other—we are a living, breathing country song."

"What? He was going to meet you here!"

"Oh! And my phone is at the bottom of the sewer drain."

My voice was high-pitched and singsongy and sounding seriously insane. "And I threw my daisy ring at him and lost it in the parking lot. The one thing I had to remind me I was his girlfriend almost. And it's lost."

"Oh, Sweetness." She put her phone down and hugged me. "Wait. My phone! We can call him with mine! What's his number?"

Serenity, the brilliant one. "Awesome! It's 2!"

"What?"

Oh no. I had put him on speed dial and 2 was all I could remember. "I . . . I don't actually know his number." I dropped my head. "Can you believe that? How could I not know his number?"

She draped her arm over me and sighed. "Stupid smart phones."

I took in a few deep breaths and pushed away the tears. It felt like Ian was fading from me. My regular sane voice came back, but it was weak. "I don't know if Ian and I are ever going to land in the same place. Why is this so hard for us? I just want what you and Mike have. I want someone to be at my hip. Someone to send me adorable texts when I'm in the same room. Someone to call me by *my* essence."

She laughed. "They do."

"They who?" "The guys, silly." She pushed back from me and we locked eyes.

"They call you Sweetness because that *is* your essence."

"Really? It's not because I'm a party girl?"

"Hell no. You're all sweetness, through and through. They've known that for a long time." She bumped shoulders with me. "And I think Ian has, too."

"Then why do we keep missing each other? Why aren't *we* human magnets?" I cried like a blubbering mess. "It's my reputation, isn't it? It'll never go away."

"What reputation, silly?"

I wiped the snot from my nose with the back of my hand. "Last summer at Jimmy DeFranco's party"—I took a deep breath, scared to tell her the rest. So I closed my eyes and let it out—"I kissed two guys in one night."

She laughed. Like a big, deep, horse laugh. "You don't even want to know what I've done with two guys in one night. Bliss and I used to play that game. I understand. I've kissed *a lot* of guys."

"But why'd you stop? Why Mike?"

"This one weekend, Bliss and I went to the lake. We were standing in line to rent inner tubes, and Mike introduced himself." She tapped her finger on her cheek, taking her time to enjoy this memory. "My hands were full, and he offered to carry mine. And that was it. Isn't that stupid? Something so small."

It wasn't stupid. I knew exactly what she meant. Ian did look good the day he wore that green shirt, it was true. But it wasn't the shirt that changed everything. It was the licorice and Motrin. He knew when I most needed help. He always gave me what I needed.

Peanut butter cookie.

Daisy ring.

That crease.

It never was the green shirt.

Serenity put her phone away and watched Mike as he filled cups and handed them out. "It's easy with Mike. All of it. I don't worry we'll run out of things to talk about. I don't worry whether or not he thinks I'm hot." She looked across the room and winked at him. "With him it is seriously no worries."

I took a deep breath, feeling the same way. With Ian, I never had worries. Not until tonight. "There has to be a reason Ian left, right?" I grabbed her by the arm. "Tell me there's a good reason."

"There's an explanation. There *always* is." She looked at me with gleaming eyes.

"Wait here. I'll go see what Mike knows." She stood, then put her hand up like a stop sign. "Don't. Move."

I sat frozen and watched Serenity walk over to Mike. But he immediately attacked her, and they started making out. It looked as though Serenity had already forgotten why she'd gone over there in the first place. Wow. Graphic.

Sitting on that love seat by myself, I felt small. Defeated. Alone. I either needed to find Ian or go home.

"Want a slice?" It was Allyson, standing at my feet as she held out a piece of pizza.

The sudden appearance of pizza near my face caused my stomach to growl like a pit bull.

I was starving, and it was veggie—the only kind I eat—but I wasn't about to take pizza presented by Allyson Moore. Because then I'd have to thank her. And make eye contact with her. And *not* inflict bodily harm on her.

No way. I couldn't do it.

But I was secretly relieved. At least she was here, in this room, and not with Ian.

"I'm glad you finally made it to the party. We were getting worried."

"*We?*" My adrenaline started flowing. I popped up off the sofa and faced her. "As in you and Ian?"

"Everyone. And yeah, Ian."

Oh, no. Here we go. "You talked to him. *You* did."

"You turned your phone off."

"So did he!"

"But he turned it back on and now he can't get a hold of you."

That was it. Some people have boundaries or lines or whatever. And this was mine. She wasn't going to talk about Ian as if she knew him better than I did. As if she had knowledge of that crease.

"I was in the bathroom at the In-N-Out Burger, Allyson. I know you've been talking to him all night."

"We were planning this." She motioned her hands across the room.

"Exactly. You were the one asking him for favors. You were making plans with *my date*!" I gritted my teeth, feeling the werewolf grow inside me.

She shook her head. "That's not it."

But I didn't want to hear one word of her worthless explanation. "Back OFF!"

She batted her eyes, stunned by my words, or maybe my growing sharp teeth, and she stood speechless.

Man, that felt good. I sat back down on the sofa, gingerly, purposefully, as if I sat on sofas for sport. But when I heard Allyson's perfect shoes walk in the other direction, I covered my face and started praying.

Help me find Ian. I need to get to him!

And then the Gods of Simplicity returned from their rafting trip and answered my prayer.

"Dude, it's tradition, we *have* to go do this. Finish what we started." Brian Sontag was in a corner, deep in discussion with this lanky guy named Boner—no one knew his real name. Apparently he got the nickname because of an incident that happened at Whitney Malone's sixth grade birthday party at a bowling alley. Something about a stuck zipper and a plate of cheese fries. I don't know. I wasn't there. But the name stuck and we've been calling him Boner ever since.

"We've got to find someone to drive." Brian shook his head. "Allyson doesn't understand."

Boner didn't say much, but seemed in agreement as he picked at his Styrofoam cup.

Serenity was now hovering next to the keg, showing her texts to anyone who'd read them. I thought she was going to find out where Ian was, but her thoughts were on Mike, not me.

I was going to have to do this myself. And this was it— my way to Ian. Brian and Boner had a car and they needed a sober driver.

I didn't know what this tradition was they were going to do, but I could still feel some werewolf left in me—my inner Ledbetter girl. I would get that car to go in the direction I needed: left out of the Hampton Inn.

To find Ian Clark.

I walked up behind Brian and whispered in his ear. "Let's go. I'll drive."

Chapter Fifteen

TAP WATER

"THAT'S MY GIRL," Gilda says, pumping her fist in the air.

"There's something else—" I try to say, but I'm interrupted when Gilda glances out the window and her face drops. Another visitor. I'm guessing from the lack of color in her face, it's not a pleasant one.

"Morning, Gilda." A fast-walking boxy woman—comfortable shoes, no makeup—charges up to the register, punches in some numbers, and opens the drawer of cash.

What in the world is going on?

Gilda must have read my mind, because she stands behind the woman and mouths to me, "The owner."

We all remain silent as the owner counts the cash and only glances up at us to flash a quick smile. By the time she gets to the twenties, the awkwardness of the moment catches up to her. "Can I help you?" She glares at Donna, who is casually sipping a Red Bull (her third of the morning), then looks over at me, comfortably perched on Gilda's stool.

"Nope," Donna says, sounding like a rebellious kid.

Oh, brother. We don't need trouble. "I've had a rough night," I explain, "and Gilda and my friend Donna were helping me figure out—"

But before I can finish, the owner rolls her eyes and spins 180 degrees to face Gilda. "How many times do we have to go over this?"

Gilda's face flushes and she nervously tugs at her braid as she motions for the owner to follow her. The two stand in the chip aisle and have a conversation, but I can only hear the owner's booming voice.

"I don't care if she had a bad time at prom. This isn't a therapist's office. You're too nice to these people, Gilda. They're customers, not friends. They have to leave."

Gilda leans in and whispers in the owner's ear. The lady steps back, squints her eyes, and looks over at me. She crosses her arms, then finally says, "Okay. But help the poor girl find a way home. And soon."

I fill a cup with tap water from the bathroom, hoping the owner sees me so she doesn't think I'm still eating complimentary junk food. But she just quietly walks back to the register, eyes down, takes out a stack of receipts, and closes the register. Before she leaves, she turns to me. "I hope you figure it out." She pats Gilda on the back and leaves.

We're all frozen. What. Just. Happened? Donna breaks the quiet by crushing her Red Bull can and tossing it into the recycling. Then she shoots Gilda a wicked smile. "So what'd you say to old crotchety pants?"

Gilda stands up straight and brushes a strand of hair back from her face. "I lied. She was going to make you leave, so I told her you needed advice." Gilda crinkles her nose, then finally says, "I told her you're gay."

I tilt my head. First left, then right. Like Sol, my Labrador. "Why'd you say that?"

"I listen to a lot of stories at this job. And I'm not supposed to socialize with the customers. She knows I don't give out advice anymore, unless it's really important. And she knows this is one issue I have a lot of experience with."

I chew at my lip. Is Gilda saying she's gay? Whatever—it doesn't matter, but—

"My daughter's gay," she says, as if she can read my mind. I'm starting to think she can. "And she went to the Ledbetter prom last night. With her girlfriend."

Of course. I remember. "Red dresses? Totally gorgeous?"

She smiles and nods, her eyes sparkling. Gilda is probably the type of mother who knows it isn't her job to pick out her daughter's dress. Or pick out *anything* for her daughter. "I can tell you this," I say. "She was *very* happy."

"I know," she says as she checks her braid again. "Finally."

I shake my head. "Gosh, I feel stupid with my heterosexual story. I don't even know why I'm bothering you with this."

Gilda walks over and gently grabs my hand. "It doesn't matter if it's a boy or a girl. With love, it's *always* complicated."

I close my eyes briefly and think of Ian's face. And his voice—so soothing. "Very."

"That's right," Donna interjects. "You just told us you agreed to be the designated driver for Brian and *Boner*?"

It's one of those questions she doesn't actually want me to answer. But this next question, she does. "Where'd they take you, doll?"

My stomach clenches at the thought of answering this. My eyes drift away from her and out the window—past the gas pumps and across the intersection and up to the jagged mountains in the distance. I secretly imagine myself living in those hills, alone. Forever. And never answering this question.

Gilda is still holding my hand. She tightens her grip as if to say, no matter what, it'll be okay. The warmth from her hand calms me. My stomach unclenches.

I can tell them.

Donna steps closer to us and squints as she stares at my dress. "Looks like we're out of stains. What happened next?"

I lift up my hand—the one Gilda's not holding. And I show them the mark. "I was bitten."

Chapter Sixteen

A THREE-LEGGED CHIHUAHUA

BRIAN'S PRIUS WAS much easier to drive than Mike's Cadillac. The blinker worked, I didn't have to crawl through anything to get to my seat, nothing caught on fire, and the seats didn't have deep leather cracks that tried to go to third base on me.

The only problem was the seating arrangement. Brian and Boner both crawled into the backseat, leaving me alone to act as chauffeur. But that was okay . . . I was now in charge of where we were headed.

I glanced in my rearview mirror, noticing how pleasantly uncracked it was. Extreme visibility. How nice.

I eased the car to the hotel exit and turned on the left blinker. "I need to find someone first."

"Take a right." Boner was looking on a map.

"But I need to go left first. If you guys don't mind...I need to find—"

Brian leaned over the seat. "Enough rights and you'll be going left." He patted my shoulder all reassuring-like.

Which it was.

"There!" Boner jammed his finger at a spot. "Huntington Drive. Let's hit 'em up!"

The guys were pumped. I wasn't sure what we were going to do, but whatever it was, these two were giddy little monsters—cackling and growling.

Kind of cute.

Huntington Drive was a couple of blocks from my house, so I knew the area well.

I turned the Prius right, out of the parking lot, and we cruised oh-so-quietly down the street. "Okay, we'll do your errand first, but then I have to get back to the other Hampton Inn. Cool?"

Neither one of them answered. They were too busy putting on dark hats and gloves.

Crap! Were we going to do something illegal? "Whoa, whoa! Please tell me we're not robbing anyone!"

"Nope." Brian pulled his gloves down tight.

"We're not vandalizing anything? Or spray painting anything?" I gripped the petite steering wheel tightly.

No answer. Now they were adjusting each other's knit hats.

I babbled on as I continued to drive, stealing glances at them in the rearview mirror. "I appreciate tradition and all, but that doesn't always make it a smart idea. I mean, on Easter we boil eggs and paint them and leave them in the yard . . . for like a *long* time. That's not sanitary. That's not smart. Tradition should be questioned sometimes. Just saying. Don't you think? Guys?"

Finally Brian leaned up to talk to me. "We're helping people." His voice was calm. "We like them to see what life is like for other people."

"That's cool. I think. Wait, how do you—"

"We . . . rearrange. That's all."

"There!" Boner's voice squeaked. "Pull up to that gray house." They both peered out the window, scoping out the place.

The house was dead—no lights. And there were no other cars around. Which wasn't shocking since it was four o'clock in the morning.

Oh my god. Four o'clock! Mom was going to kill me.

Please be a deep sleeper tonight, Mom.

"Looks like it's a six-footer," Brian said. "Hook latch. Opens from the outside. Yeah. Perfect."

Boner cracked his knuckles. "They're definitely caging something big behind that sucker."

I turned back to them. "What do you mean, *caging?*"

They ignored my question. "Stay here," Brian said in an eerily calm voice. "Leave

the engine running. This will only take a sec." Then he shoved Boner out the door. "Go!"

They scrambled out of the car, falling twice on the lawn when Brian tripped over

Boner's big feet. They'd clearly hit up the keg one too many times at that party. Once they both stopped laughing and shushing each other, they managed to unlatch the fence.

They disappeared, and within seconds I heard a yelp. And then another yelp. After the third yelp, they re-emerged, Brian with a package tucked inside his tuxedo coat.

As they jumped into the backseat, Brian scooped the package from his jacket and placed it on the front seat next to me.

A Chihuahua. He was shivering. Or maybe it was a she? He/she was adorable. Almost pathetic. It only had three legs. The spot where the front left leg should be was just a mess of fur and a rumpled scar. "You stole this dog? This little, sweet, three-legged dog?"

"It's not sweet." Brian's voice was no longer overly calm. "Drive!"

"Where?" I punched on the gas.

"Up on the right," he said, calming down but still barking out orders. "That white house on the left. Chain-link fence."

I stepped on the brake, slowing the car down. "Wait. You guys are dog swapping?"

Brian sighed, like he was relieved. "Awesome, right? You've done this before?"

"No! I have not *swapped dogs* before! This is ridiculous! This poor, sweet, little dog." I reached over and lifted the tag on his collar. His name was Chompers McGee. "Aww. He's so—"

Suddenly I learned how he got his name.

Chomp!

"Oooowwww! He bit me!!!"

"That sucker's fierce, man," Boner said with a pained look on his face. "No wonder they stash him behind a six-footer."

"It may be somewhat illegal"—Brian leaned up next to my ear and gently wrapped the silk handkerchief from his tuxedo pocket around my finger—"but I'll guarantee you when they find their dog, they're gonna spoil it with treats and let him sleep wherever he wants. They won't take him for granted anymore." I saw him smile big in the rearview mirror. "We're like modern-day Robin Hoods. Or Robin Hounds." He laughed.

I rubbed at my freshly wrapped wound and finally managed to stop the bleeding by pressing on it with the soft cloth. The pain quickly dissipated, as though Brian's cloth had healing powers. Or maybe I was ignoring the pain and concentrating on the adorable explanation Brian had just given on the profound importance of dog-swapping. Robin Hounds? Okay, that was cute.

Boner relaxed his face as he leaned back in his seat. "Plus, it's funny, dude. We're swapping dogs, bro!"

The guys high-fived.

Brian leaned over the seat again. "Yeah, and earlier tonight"— his arms dangled next to mine, and I could smell his cologne, which I normally hate on a guy, but this cologne seemed to be drawing me toward him—"we hit up a bunch of houses on the way to prom."

It was a spicy cologne, but with a sweet overtone. Like raspberries and cayenne. "Uh-huh," I said in a sort of daze.

"We swapped Great Danes, Labradors, Jack Russell terriers . . ."

I took a deep breath, a little deeper than normal, Brian's smell making me feel relaxed. "Uh-huh."

"But Allyson made us stop. She didn't get the whole Robin Hound thing. You're so cool for doing this." Brian touched my shoulder.

I liked it. But it also jerked me back to reality. I was in a car with Brian Sontag, not Ian. We were having a conversation, and I was not doing a good job keeping up. I was trying to smell him. Boy smells made me dumb. I cleared my throat and sat up straighter. "Why'd Allyson make you stop?"

Brian sat back and shook his head. "That girl doesn't get tradition."

Even though it was the most ridiculous tradition I'd ever seen two drunk guys conjure up, I had to admit, the level of cuteness about the whole thing could not be ignored.

We drove Chompers to his new temporary home, three houses away—a house that belonged to a golden retriever named Bubbles. Seriously? We couldn't have picked Bubbles up first?

We swapped two more dogs, then drove one street over. Brian cracked open a beer he'd swiped from the party. Boner counted how many seconds it took him to down it. Eleven.

Apparently, this was the other part of the tradition— slamming beers after each swap. They clearly needed a hobby. And some maturity. And a designated driver.

We swapped a German shepherd for a shih tzu. A pit bull for a poodle. An Irish setter for a springer spaniel—which wasn't much of a swap, if you ask me, because both breeds are hyper and wiggly, which was why I'd convinced Mom to go with a Labrador retriever. They are even tempered. They don't complain. They don't like confrontation. And they bring stuff back to you.

I decided it was time to talk them out of the next swap and go back to the Hampton Inn, where hopefully Ian was waiting for me, because Brian's once-adorable explanation had denigrated to a drunken, "We're teaching people to appreciate life, and crap like that."

"I have to get back to the hotel."

"No! More swaps!" Brian and Boner yelped and laughed and burped and pumped their fists in the air.

They were tanked. And I needed to go get my Ian. "Sorry guys. The field trip's over." I pulled the car into a driveway to turn around, and I saw headlights coming down the street. The lights slowed a few houses away from us and pulled into a driveway. As it made the turn, I could see it was a limo.

Brianna's limo. "Oh, no."

"What is it?" Brian and Boner scrambled to sit up straight enough to see out. The three of us watched in silence as the limo driver—my so-called parking-lot therapist who had me convinced Ian *wasn't* interested—opened the back door and out fell a clearly drunk Brianna with Allyson steadying her by the arm.

"Oh, boy—here we go," Brian said softly.

The two of them made it almost halfway up the driveway before Allyson glanced in our direction. Her annoyed face revealed that she recognized the Prius.

"What are you *doing*, Brian?!" she yelled, throwing her arms in the air, which caused Brianna to stumble around without her support.

Brian popped open the back door, but paused to look at me with a helpless face, like a runaway stray dog. "Come with me, Justina. I'll explain everything to her."

Allyson and Brianna stormed over, Brianna holding her hand out to an invisible rail to keep herself steady. We met them halfway, on a neighbor's lawn, dampened with early morning dew.

"Lookie. It's Justina," Brianna slurred. "And she's with two guys. Whatta shocker!"

Before I could answer, Allyson jumped Brian with the mother of all lectures. "How dare you leave me at that party. I had no ride home and someone could have slipped me a roofie and I'd be dead and embarrassed somewhere if it weren't for this limo driver, you jerk! And tell me you did *not* go out and swap more dogs. That illegal, you know!"

"Sorry, babe." Brian leaned over and gave her a quick peck on the forehead. "Call me later."

"Fine."

"Fine."

And that was it.

That was it? That was his entire explanation?!

He sauntered back to the car and fell into the backseat without a care in the world.

And there I was alone on a damp lawn at five o'clock in the morning, face-to-face with Evil #1 and Evil #2.

I wanted to melt like a stick of butter, but I couldn't. I was going to have to deal with this. "It's not what you think," I said.

"It *is* what we think." Allyson crossed her arms and put on her best I-would-never-do-something-so-bad face. "You left a party with two guys, Justina. And one of them was my date!"

Which, truthfully, did sound pretty bad. Why hadn't I told someone where I was going? "I swear, Allyson. I was just—"

"Your reputation isn't going anywhere, is it?" Brianna stepped closer to my face, her vodka breath making me nauseous. "No one wants to date you, Justina. They just want to party with you. Face it."

I turned my face away, and my body flushed with anger. And shame. But they didn't know the truth—I was trying to find Ian.

Where are you, Ian? Please swoop in. Please.

"Go wait by the limo." Allyson nudged Brianna away. "I'll deal with this."

Brianna threw her fireworks finale of hurtful words at me as she staggered away. "Love all the stains on your dress! You shoulda worn black so you could cover 'em up with a Sharpie! Hahaha!" She approached the limo and reached out to the trunk to hold herself up, but puked by the back tire.

Tears dripped down my face. I could barely get the words out to tell Allyson. "I wasn't trying to take Brian from you. I . . . I thought you were trying to take Ian."

She pressed her lips together, not like she was mad, but like she was holding back. She sighed. "It's not what you think, Justina. He doesn't have feelings for me like he does for you. Do you even know how lucky you are?"

She tugged at her ponytail nervously. "That guy deserves . . ." She paused, her eyes reddening. I could almost see the wheels in her head turning—she was thinking about him. I understood the painful expression that sprawled across her face—I'd had that look before, too. She glanced down at my hand—more precisely at my bare, ringless finger. She bit her lip, looking unsure as to whether she should finish her thought. But she did. "Ian deserves someone who will accept what he has to give."

I considered telling her how I found the ring and bought it, and how my mom was going to kill me for spending so much money. . . .

But then I realized it wasn't important.

Here I was wasting all this time wondering how he would kiss me, wondering if he'd loop pinkies with me when we walked down the hall . . . wondering if he was truly boyfriend material.

When the truth was, I wasn't girlfriend material.

I couldn't face Ian. I had ruined this night. I had ruined everything with him. He'd tried to make me his girlfriend and I'd rejected him. I went to prom with him and ended up kissing one guy and leaving with two others. There was no apology for that. No note scribbled out on a napkin would make up for not being the girl he hoped for. He deserved better . . . and Allyson should be the one to tell him.

I rubbed my bare finger. "You're right, Allyson. He deserves someone special. He deserves better. Tell him I'm sorry." I spun around to go back to the car. But as much as I knew deep down that I wasn't what Ian deserved . . . still . . . I *had* to know. I whipped back around. "Allyson?"

She turned to face me. "Yeah?"

"Did you ever see the crease?"

"The what?"

"The face he gives when you go back and forth with him and it almost goes too far—he pulls his mouth up to the right. There's a crease there. Did you ever see it?"

She crossed her arms and let out a deep sigh. She looked defeated. "No. I never noticed it."

I clutched at my stomach. I had hoped it was true. That lovely, tiny thing was just for me. "Thanks," I said, my voice weak and quivering. "I . . . I just needed to know."

I don't know what difference it made to me, I just knew it did.

But Ian and I didn't seem to be able to land in the same spot at the right precise moment. This night symbolized everything between us—we kept slipping by each other.

So I turned and went back to the car, back to Brian, back to my past.

I could hear Allyson's beautiful shoes behind me, retreating up Brianna's driveway. When I reached the car, Brian held the back door open for me. "We're done swapping. Let's go for a drive."

"But you guys need a designated driver," I said.

"Boner doesn't drink."

"But what about all that falling down?"

"He's clumsy." Brian pointed to Boner's unusually large feet. And so Boner drove as we cruised the back streets blaring AC/DC with the windows down. My hair was flying as Brian and I screamed the lyrics at the top of our lungs.

"Hey," Brian said as he reached over and put his hand on top of mine. He kept bouncing his head along to the song, then leaned in and yelled so I could hear him. "Prom sucked."

I nodded. He put his arm around me. Warm. Strong. Oh, God. What was happening? I took a deep breath because I knew I needed to slap him for hitting on me when he was supposed to be with Allyson. But the air filled with the smell of raspberries and cayenne. And boy smells made me do things I regret.

Ian deserved a better girl—and it wasn't me.

Brian pushed over and got closer.

Chapter Seventeen
DOUBLE STUF OREOS

GILDA AND DONNA have blank looks. They aren't speaking. No squinting. No head tilting. Nothing. I can't tell if they are shocked or if they've been frozen. "Should I keep going?" I ask.

Gilda finally clears her throat. But still, nothing.

Donna finally opens her mouth. Then she takes a deep breath. "Let me get this straight—you got together with *Brian*?"

"There's more to it. I got swept up—"

"But you knew what that would do to Ian," Gilda says, as if she's defending him, as if she knows him.

"But Ian—"

"Okay, look, doll," Donna interrupts. "You don't have to deprive yourself. A woman has a right to enjoy a man's mouth. It's constitutional."

I nod.

"But all we're saying is maybe you didn't think through the consequences of your actions."

I throw my arms in the air, frustrated that they seem to be suddenly taking his side. "But you are the one who keeps calling him Captain Scumbag."

"Well, sure. I guess. He is a *guy*, but—" Donna shakes her head.

"But what? I'm not the girl for him? He deserves better?"

Gilda clasps her hands together as if she's praying. "Couldn't you have waited until you had some questions answered?"

"Like?"

Donna paces the floor. "Like why was he driving away from the hotel when you got there?"

"And why did he turn his phone off?" Gilda adds.

Then the Questioning Firing Squad unloads on me.

"And what did his text mean?"

"Why did he call you his girlfriend if he didn't mean it?"

"*Did* he mean it?"

"Why did Serenity leave you sitting there? Is she really a friend to you?"

"And why did he leave you at prom in the first place?"

"Justina?"

I feel dizzy. Not in a low-blood-sugar way, but in a I-thought-I-was-right-but-maybe-I-was-wrong kind of way. I cover my face and blabber through my fingers. "I don't know. You're right. I should've waited. I should've given him one more chance to explain." My shoulders slump as I clutch my stomach. "But I guess I just went back to being The Girl At That Party. It felt comfortable. It was easy." I swallow hard and cut my eyes back up at them. "But you don't understand . . . there's more." Before they can fire more questions at me, the bell rings.

"Dude! They have Double Stuf Oreos!" It's the Mikes. The Mikes have walked into the store.

THE MIKES HAVE WALKED INTO THE STORE!!!

I leap off my stool and sprint over to the candy aisle, charging them like a galloping antelope. "Mike! MIKE!"

They startle and stare at me a moment before my face slowly registers in their sloshed brains. "Sweetness!" Mike grabs me by the shoulders. "Where have you been?! We've been driving all over town looking for you!"

"I . . . I . . ." This story is too long. It's too complicated. I have no idea where to begin, so I don't. "Where's Serenity? And Bliss?"

"Bliss is passed out in the car, and Serenity is . . . well, let's just say you have seriously messed with her essence. She's not serene anymore."

"Oh my god! You're *here*?!" Serenity bursts through the door and wraps me up in her arms. But they aren't loving arms—they're tight, smothering arms, like she won't let go.

Mike leans into our tangle of a hug. "Serenity's been on a freaking rampage trying to find you."

Despite the smothering, her embrace is warm and strong. It feels so nice to be protected. I have known Serenity for only ten hours, but I have a sense she would defend me forever. I can't help but cry. "I'm so sorry."

"It's okay," she whispers in my ear. "Ian is okay, too. I'm just glad you're safe."

I push back and grab her hands. "Ian? What do you mean? You saw him?!"

The mere mention of Ian immediately draws Gilda and Donna over to us. Donna puts her hand on my shoulder, as if to claim me as her own, and glares at Serenity. "So you're the one they call Serenity?"

She narrows her eyes. "Who are you?"

"I'm the one who dispenses good advice. Like a friend would do."

"I've been telling them what happened," I explain.

Donna draws her eyebrows together. "You know where Captain Scumbag is, huh?"

"Captain Scumbag?" Serenity looks confused.

"Ian," I explain. "I told them all about it. What he did to me. Do you know where he is?"

"He came back to the hotel right after you left. You should've waited, Justina. He's not a scumbag." She crosses her arms over her chest and looks directly at Donna. "Not even close."

I step back from her, trying to read her face. "What do you mean?"

"He told me everything . . . why he left . . . what those phone calls to Allyson were about. He was getting her to help him surprise you. That party at the Hampton Inn was supposed to be for you—and he knew you'd be hungry so he got Allyson to order those pizzas."

"Dude, those pizzas were disgusting," Other Mike offers. "All veggie."

Oh no. No, no, no. The pizza slice Allyson offered me— that pizza . . . was for *me*?

Of course it was: only *he* would know to order me veggie pizza.

I look over at Donna, and she mouths the words "Parasite Pal." And she was right. Allyson would do anything for me—even if it meant being the one to organize a pizza party at the Hampton Inn—as long as she could be closer to him. Or at least someone *like* him. And could I really blame her?

"But there's more. The reason he left the prom—he was doing a favor"—Serenity takes a deep breath and winces— "for your mother."

"He . . . wait. What? Did you say my *mother*?" Oh, this can't be happening. Mom and I were getting somewhere. She was trying to stop being so involved in my life. But *this*? This was the opposite of uninvolved. This was extreme involvement. This was child abuse! "She asked him for a favor . . . on my *prom night*?!" I yell, my voice screeching so high Gilda covers her ears.

"Calm down." Serenity turns to Mike. "I knew this wouldn't go well."

He shakes his head and motions to Other Mike to hand over an Oreo for comfort. Other Mike is sitting down in the cookie aisle, legs crossed, snacking.

Serenity snatches a cookie from him and places it in my hand. "Look, it was your dog."

"Sol?"

"Something about your mom coming home and finding a Great Dane in your backyard and your dog was missing."

Oh my god. Brian and Boner. They said they had hit up a bunch of houses before prom. They swapped Sol for a Great Dane!

"She knew you'd lose it if anything happened to your dog, and apparently she tried to call the dog pound and the police and the FBI, but she couldn't get any help. So she called Ian. Did you tell her she could call him with emergencies or something? Tell me you didn't actually say those words to her, did you?"

I drop my head.

"Aw, Sweetness." She puts her arm around me. "There's no way you could've known she thought you *meant* it." Serenity shuffles and takes a step back. "But it doesn't make sense. I mean, who the hell would swap a dog?"

"I know who," I say under my breath as I drop my head again. But before I can explain, she goes on.

"He told me he only thought he'd be gone for half an hour, but when the other neighbors started realizing their dogs were gone too, they asked him to help. The poor guy had to find like eight dogs." She pops a cookie in her mouth. "Then later there were a whole bunch of other dogs that got swapped, and his phone kept ringing to help find them, so that's why he turned his phone off."

I feel sick. This is all too much. I thought I had pulled all the facts together. It seemed to be the only conclusion. But the truth was he was out taking dogs to their homes—and I was helping Brian swap them.

Only you could never say no to my mom. Only you would spend prom night doing favors for my entire neighborhood.

"He's been looking for you." Serenity lowers her voice. "But I had to tell him you left the party. With Brian."

"What? Why'd you tell him that?"

"I had to! We didn't know what happened to you. I told you to sit there and wait for me, but you didn't! If you would've waited just five minutes, all the questions would've been answered. But you left with two other guys? Why Justina?"

I kneel by the Oreo display and cry quietly to myself, for the millionth time of the night, hoping all these people around me, as well-meaning as they are, will disappear.

Serenity kneels down next to me. "What were you doing?"

"We were dog swapping."

"What?!"

"I tried to stop them at first, but they convinced me they were doing it for the good of mankind, and then it turned out to be so much fun, and I was hungry and I made bad decisions. . . ." I babble and cry like a lunatic. "I was trying to find Ian—I was. But the truth is, I *did* leave with two other guys. And no matter what my intentions were"—I shake my head at the thought of what I've done—"intentions don't matter. Ian deserves so much better—"

"Stop crying, Sweetness." Mike kneels down next to us.

"I'm sorry. We were just so worried." Serenity brushes her hand across my forehead, not knowing there's a growing knot there. I wince in pain. "What's wrong?" she asks.

I lift my head and look up at Gilda and Donna as I push back my hair to reveal the knot. "I haven't explained everything yet."

Chapter Eighteen
BRIAN SONTAG

HIS COLOGNE WAS strong—raspberries and cayenne. It was mixed with the smell of beer.

But I ignored the beer part.

I felt so relaxed. And out of my mind. What was happening?

The radio was still blaring and I had to nuzzle near his ear so he could hear me. "What about Allyson?"

He shrugged. "Don't care."

I sat up. "Why?" Boner must have noticed we were trying to have a conversation, because he turned the music down to a bearable level.

"She drives me crazy," Brian said. "All she does is talk."

I remembered her cornering Ian at Dan's house. "She definitely uses her hands a lot when she talks," I said. "High drama."

"Tell me about it. It's nonstop. All she wants to talk about is flag corps and yearbook meetings and prom planning committees."

The poor guy. I couldn't imagine having to listen to her meaningless stories.

Brian looked at me, his eyes happy and gleaming. Or maybe it was the alcohol-induced haze. "What about Ian?"

I shrugged. "Don't care." Which was a lie and I couldn't believe the words had come out of my mouth so easily.

Brian laughed and pulled me in close to him.

He certainly didn't seem concerned about Allyson, but he was also totally drunk. Which was why I had an urge to resist him—drunk guys are not my favorite kind. But my resistance was quickly overpowered by my need to smell more of that cologne.

I inhaled deeply and felt a little woozy. Kind of intoxicated—like I couldn't think quite straight. He squeezed tighter and I exhaled, caving into his body.

I wanted to kiss Brian. Or maybe I just wanted to kiss *someone*, but Brian was the one with his strong arms around me, giving off an irresistible smell.

But this would be it. If I kissed Brian, I would lose Ian.

I told him I would never choose to kiss someone if we were together. It was my choice. Kiss Brian and end it with Ian. Lose our friendship.

Lose everything.

And I knew this wouldn't turn into anything with Brian. We'd kiss, then he'd become a number on my very long list. But this was how it worked for me, this was the routine. Brianna was right—reputations can't be erased. And Ian deserved someone far better than me. Some girls are The Girl. Not me. I am The Girl At That Party. Always have been. And for tonight, I would be again.

I looked up at Brian. "Kiss me."

His eyes grew wide. "Yeah?"

I liked that he wanted to make sure. "Yeah."

Just as he leaned into me, I put my hands on his cheeks and pulled back slightly. "I'm kind of nervous, but I want you to know—"

He put his finger up to my lips. "Shhh."

He wiped my hair from my face and put his lips near my neck. I could feel his breath. It sent a tingle through my body.

"I can't believe I'm doing this," I said. "You probably don't know that I haven't kissed a guy in eight months, twelve days."

He breathed harder. "Shhh."

More tingling, but I wanted him to know this. He needed to know what he was getting into and why this kiss was ridiculously huge for me. I took a deep breath. "No, seriously. This is important."

He moved his mouth up closer to my ear and whispered, "Stop talking. Don't ruin this."

I pushed back, wriggling out of his grasp. "*Ruin* it?"

"Dude, come on. This doesn't have to be so complicated. We don't have to talk. That's all Allyson ever wants to do." He threw his head back and stared at the ceiling. "Just kiss me."

Oh crap. It made sense to me now why Allyson wanted to talk to Ian so badly. Maybe it wasn't right for her to get my potential future boyfriend to listen to her, but maybe she just wanted *someone* to listen to her. I doubted Brianna was offering much in the way of meaningful conversation. And Brian seemed to have only one thing on his mind.

Then the biology of the situation hit me—our human needs. Food. Shelter. Great kissing. And a need to feel special—different from all the other humans running around.

And that's what Ian did for me. The fact that Ian and I had been existing and orbiting each other in this world without meeting, and then found each other on the curb that night in our darkest moments . . . it was not an accident. Our relationship was the stuff of stars—big, incomprehensible.

Allyson wanted that. Who wouldn't?

"Seriously." Brian leaned his heavy body on mine, smelling more like beer now, not cologne. "Kiss me, would you?"

I turned my head from him and quickly weighed the consequences. I could've pulled a Hailey—roll and deflect. I could've been polite and gotten out of the situation gracefully, and we would've driven back to the party without a problem. But Brian needed to hear this. No matter what the consequences were.

"You know what, Brian? You may think Allyson talks too much, but all that stuff's important to her. It *is* her. And you don't want to hear it? Maybe flag corps and the yearbook sound stupid to you, but all I ever talk about to Ian is my over-involved mother and stories about Christmas and why I love daisies. I'm just as stupid."

Brian rolled his eyes, clearly annoyed. "Stop, Justina. I'm not talking about this."

But I wasn't stopping. "And he listens to it. All of it. Ian makes me feel like the most special person on Earth." My voice cracked.

He rubbed at his eyes like he wanted to rub away this moment. But I swallowed hard, kept it together, and drove it home. "And see this dress? This nasty, stain-covered dress? I got it at a second-hand store. It cost as much as a case of Capri Sun. And my mother loved the beauty of a rose that matched a dress. She actually said those words. I have a mother who actually says stuff like that! How lucky am I? It's because of her that I don't look like any of the other Huntington High girls tonight—because I'm *not* like the rest of them. This dress *is* me. And Ian is the one who seems to get that."

He shook his head. "Jesus, I need a beer. You done now?"

"Did you hear a word I said?"

He sat up and turned his body to face me. "What happened to you?"

I pressed my head into the back of the seat, unsure what he was talking about. "You and Hailey. You two have kissed half our school. Why'd you stop the game?"

That. The Reputation. Of course.

"It's not a game anymore," I said under my breath, hoping he wouldn't hear me because this was the part of the conversation I did *not* want to be having.

"You two were a sure thing. You still are, right?" He leaned in to catch my eye. "You can't just change your reputation because you want to. It follows you . . . and guys assume . . ." His voice trailed off.

I turned and faced the window—the sun was just starting to lighten the sky. I knew Mom was going to kill me for staying out all night, but I was more focused on making sure Brian couldn't see my eyes fill with tears. I didn't want him to feel sorry for me.

He huffed. "Look, are we going to do this, or what? We all know you're not the type of girl who can resist."

I whipped my head back to face him. "I'm *not* that same girl. I'd rather kiss no one than kiss a *nobody*." I wiped my face and pushed my shoulders back. "Let me out of this car."

"Why? Ian's not here. He left you."

"Let me out!"

Boner slowed the car. "What's going on?"

Brian leaned up to him. "Don't stop. We're going back to the hotel." He sat back and looked forward with a cold stare. "I'm sure your boyfriend's waiting for you. Right?"

But he was wrong. I knew every inch of Ian's brain and how his mind worked. "Ian's *not* waiting for me." I clenched my teeth. "He's *looking* for me."

"Not when he finds out you ditched him to be with me. We all know Ian Clark doesn't put up with cheaters." He put his hand on my knee and fiddled with the hem of my dress—teasing, testing.

"Stop the car!" I screamed.

Boner started to slow again, and Brian put his hand on his shoulder. "Go."

But I knew I couldn't trust him to get where I needed to go. Finding Ian was in my own hands. Before Boner could hit the gas, I popped the door handle, thrust my body forward, tucked and rolled, and landed on the ground. In a ditch.

Only I didn't actually tuck and roll. I tumbled and flopped and landed with a *thunk* on the hard ground, with my forehead serving as a cushion for my fall.

Ouch!

And there I was, a heap of a disgusting mess, lying in a ditch on the side of Hollister Road at 6:15 a.m.

Without Ian. Without my ring. But it was clear I still had my reputation. It seemed I would never escape that. And Ian had every right to think I was up to my old tricks. I had to face the facts—I had ditched him for another guy because I assumed he didn't want to be with me.

I screwed everything up. I had lost Ian. The one guy who wanted to be my boyfriend. And I never even got a kiss.

Eight months, thirteen days.

And counting.

CHAPTER NINETEEN

MRS. FIELDS PEANUT
BUTTER COOKIE

"HOW WAS I supposed to know he was throwing a party for *me*?" I yell like a lunatic, as if yelling like a lunatic will solve my problem now.

Gilda looks concerned.

Donna sighs. Mike shrugs his shoulders.

Other Mike breaks into a bag of Bugles.

Serenity is smiling.

I look around and take in their faces, so thankful I have this group of people here for me—this ragtag, bizarre, wonderful group of people. There is kindness in my life. And it's all around me right now. I take a deep breath. "Thank you," I say softly.

And even though I ruined my chances with Ian, I feel satisfied that it's all over. This horrible night is finally past me. I'm done.

I wipe the tears from my face and lift my chin to them. "Now . . . can someone give me a ride home?"

Serenity scoops me back up in her arms and leads me to the door.

I stop and turn back to Gilda and Donna. "Thanks. For everything."

Gilda rushes up to me and smothers me with a hug, and I whisper in her ear, "I'm not going to be The Girl At That Party anymore."

She steps back and cups my chin. "You never were."

It's true. I'm not that girl anymore. And there will be a time when I'll be The Girl. It *is* all about timing—and one day when I'm not planning it, and organizing it and strangling it, love will become possible. There won't be any more leapfrogging. We'll land in the exact spot at the same precise moment. And I will wait.

Ian and I missed our moment. But I'm glad we got close. As elusive and improbable as love is . . . I got *that* close. Amazing, really.

Donna steps up to me. She doesn't put her hands on my shoulders like a football coach. She clasps my hands instead and says in a soft voice, "I'm not really a cougar."

"I know, Donna."

She bites at her lip. "And they're not *all* scumbags."

I nod.

Her eyes are watery. "I just seem to have a way of scaring the good ones off, doll."

I squeeze her hands tighter. "You'll find a good one. If you're looking for one."

She lets go and lifts her arms like she's going to hug me, so I lift mine too, ready to embrace her. But instead of hugging it out, she struts right past me and stands guard by the window. She tilts her head as if she hears something.

And then we all hear it. A rumble.

Not my stomach. I'm finally not hungry anymore. In fact, I'm so stuffed I think I'll never eat again.

It's a different rumble. A familiar one. The rattling, clanging sound of a diesel engine.

Donna presses her hand up to the window. "O.M.God . . . Captain Scumbag . . . he's here."

From the window, I watch as Ian's car pulls into the lot. He barely even gets it into park before jumping out and barreling toward the 7-Eleven.

His tux is filthy—full of stains—and his Converse high- tops are covered in mud. Then I notice his eyes, bleary and bloodshot, but it's his eyebrows that tell me what he's feeling: worry.

As he comes toward me, Ian looks up, and through the glass, our eyes meet. He suddenly stops in his tracks in the middle of the parking lot.

I grab my chest—I'm barely breathing.

But his eyes immediately light up, and his right eyebrow arches and lifts to the sky.

Oh, thank God. I know that one. It's his relieved face.

And here you are, Ian Clark, swooping in to save me. In the parking lot of the 7-Eleven.

I bolt out of the store like a cheetah and race up to him. He opens his mouth, but before he can talk, I start. "I'm so sorry, I had no idea," I babble, high-pitched and squeaky. "I thought you were trying to get together with Allyson, not planning a pizza party for me, and you turned off your phone so I thought you didn't want to be with me—"

He grabs me. Hugs me. Pulls me in tight. "It's okay."

"No. It's not." I push back from him, taking in his soft face. It's this face that I've looked at for so long, grateful for its sweetness. And I realize deep down that I am grateful for the friendship. And then deep, deep down, grateful for the electricity his touch gives me. "I was wrong. I assumed horrible things, Ian."

"And you think that's shocking to me?" He laughs. That goofy laugh that gives me butterflies.

This softness, this forgiveness, it is my hugest relief. He's here. He's laughing. I don't understand this one bit. "How did you find me?"

"I called Brian Sontag."

I drop my head, ashamed of what I've done. Worried this is the part where he tells me he doesn't ever want to talk to me again.

"Brian explained what happened . . . the dog swapping . . . you trying to kiss him."

I snap my head up. "But—"

"And he told me about you *not* kissing him. And then about you jumping out of the car on Lexington Avenue to come find me. Are you nuts, Justina?" He lifts my chin with his hand. "Don't answer that."

He reaches into his pocket. "I found this in the parking lot of the Hampton Inn."

My Muppet-looking daisy ring.

"Serenity told me you bought it back from Fritz." My fingers tremble as he slides the ring on and grabs my hand tight. "It fits you perfectly."

And he's right. It fits me in every way.

There are so many things I've wanted to tell him, but haven't. Here he was, the one guy who listened to everything I had to say, and I couldn't tell him how I felt about *him*.

"I've never told you about the green shirt," I blurt out.

"The what?" "A few weeks ago, you came to my house in a new green shirt, and I thought that was what made me have feelings for you." My hands start to shake. He grabs them, holds them still, our fingers interlacing. "But what I realized tonight was it wasn't the shirt. It was way before that. The silver bat. And then the Motrin. And the licorice and the peanut butter cookie."

He tilts his head and gives me a curious smile. "Silver bat?"

"The first day we met, playing softball in gym class, you handed me that bat—handle first." I squeeze his hands tighter, and my voice quivers. "I've had feelings for you ever since I met you, Ian Clark."

We both take a deep breath, realizing we're saying all the things we are finally ready to say.

"I've had feelings for you for a long time, too," he says, then leans in, forcing me to look up at him. He has a sneaky smirk on his face. "Didn't you ever wonder why the silver bat was always around after that day?"

I shake my head and laugh. *Of course* he'd be the one to make sure my favorite bat was always around.

"I don't know why we missed each other tonight," he says. "And my biggest regret is that I left you. But I found you." He holds my gaze, gently pulls his fingers through my wild hair—just like in my ridiculous fantasy—and pulls me into him as he whispers in my ear, "And I'm not letting you go."

And that's the moment when the music in the gas station parking lot, which usually blares country songs, suddenly changes to a new song. Our song. "Open Arms."

I look toward the store and Gilda is standing in the window, watching us, arms folded. Waiting.

This moment is dripping in cheesiness—epic, huge, Hummer-like cheesiness. But at least it's the nacho kind— only the best for my guy.

Donna mouths, "Kiss the scumbag!"

It's not the moment I'd imagined—no kissing under an umbrella with the stars falling around us. But here, this moment, in the parking lot of the 7-Eleven. . . it was the most perfect kiss I could ever hope for.

Before I can ready my stance and prepare for The Moment of Lip Lock Bliss, he lays it on me.

O.M.God.

He sure knows when to slow things down. And when to step on the gas.

I finally know which category you belong in, Ian Clark.

We pull back from each other, taking a deep breath, silently recognizing what has just become of our friendship. And that's when I see it. The right side of his mouth pulls up, and there it is—the crease.

All mine. And I can breathe.

"Come on, Captain." I stick my finger out, and we loop pinkies. "I have some people who want to meet you."

But before the door slides open, he pulls out a crushed Mrs. Fields peanut butter cookie from his pocket. "You must be hungry."

I'm not hungry one bit. But I will never turn away another gift from you, Ian Clark. Ever.

"Thanks," I say as I take the cookie from him. "I'm starving."

THE FOLLOWING FRIDAY

(WRITTEN ON A napkin from the nacho cheese bar at the 7-Eleven, not the sucky 7-Eleven near downtown, the one on 4th and Hill . . . the awesome one)

Dear Ian,

I will never leave your side again, not even if a dress malfunction leaves me nude. Not even if veggie pizza is being served in the girls' bathroom. Not even if Journey themselves are playing in the parking lot. I will forever be the human blueberry attached to your hip. Your personal refrigerator magnet. And I'm glad I now know that when you mentioned "weirdness," you meant "excessive making out." Um, wow. Graphic.

Hither and dither, perfunctory and whatnot. Anderson Cooper can eat your dust.

Love, Justina
(Your girlfriend)
(Yep. I'm gonna go ahead and make that assumption.)

ACKNOWLEDGMENTS

A shout-out to the late, great movie maker, John Hughes. Thank you for shaping my formative years. For showing me that every teenager has a story. It's often funny, often heartbreaking, and often there is love. And we should pay attention. Because in the words of Ferris Bueller, "Life moves pretty fast. If you don't stop and look around once in a while, you could miss it."

FOR YOU, DEAR READER

Thank you for reading PERFECT KISS. I hope you enjoyed reading as much as I enjoyed writing it. This was the most organic writing experience I've ever had. Typically, I outline my novels to death. But for this one, all I knew was how it started and how it ended. Everything in between was made up on the spot. Each day I'd write myself into a corner, then tell Robin-Of-Tomorrow to figure it out. Honestly, it was an absolute blast.

So what's next? I have a couple of projects I'm working on. It would be so helpful to hear from readers though…what would you like to read next?

Are you interested in another teen romantic comedy? Or would you rather read a New Adult romantic comedy about a girl dealing with life after graduating from college?

Send me a note letting me know what you'd love to see next from me!

Email: robinmellombooks@gmail.com

Twitter: @robinmellom

Website: www.robinmellom.com

Made in the USA
Lexington, KY
06 June 2015